the word, *manfully* – as with openers. It has always seemed to me that
l just get that bit right the rest would follow automatically. I thought of tl
sentence as a kind of semantic womb stuffed with the busy little embryos
itten pages, brilliant little nugget [illegible] practically panting to be bo
that grand vessel the entire st[illegible] orth. Wha
ion! Exactly the opposite was tru[illegible] en't any go
Savor this, for example: 'When [illegible] Morris Mc
even before picking up the rec[illegible] dame, and
something else too: dames meant trouble.' Or this: 'Just before being hack
eces by Gamel's sadistic soldiers, Colonel Benchley had a vision of the lit
ewashed cottage in Shropshire, and Mrs Benchley in the doorway, and the c
' Or this: 'Paris, London, Djibouti, all seemed unreal to him now he sat an
uins of yet another Thanksgiving dinner with his mother and father and t
Charles.' Who can remain unimpressed by sentences like these? They are
nant with meaning, so, I dare say, poignant with it that they positively bu
whole unwritten chapters – unwritten, but there, already there!

as, in reality they were nothing but bubbles, illusions every one. Each of
lerful phrases, so full of promise, was like a gift-wrapped box clutched i
child's eager hand, a box that holds nothing but gravel and bits of tra
gh it rattles oh so enticingly. He thinks it is candy! I thought it was literatu
iose sentences – and many, many others as well – proved to be not spri
ls to the great unwritten novel but insurmountable barriers to it. You s
were too good. I could never live up to them. Some writers can never eq
first novel. I could never equal my first sentence. And look at me now. Lo
I have begun this, my final work, my opus: 'I had always imagined that
ory, if and when…' Good God, 'if and when'! You see the problem. Hopele
ch it. I had always imagined that my life story, if and when I wrote it, wo
a great first line: something lyric like Nabokov's 'Lolita, light of my life, f
y loins'; or if I could not do lyric, then something sweeping like Tolstoy's
y families are alike, but every unhappy family is unhappy in its own wa
e remember those words even when they have forgotten everything e
the books. When it comes to openers, though, the best in my view has to
eginning of Ford Madox Ford's The Good Soldier: 'This is the saddest stor
ever heard.' I've read that one dozens of times and it still knocks my socks
Madox Ford was a Big One. In my life struggling to write I have strugg
nothing so manfully – yes, that's the word, manfully – as with openers. It
s seemed to me that if I could just get that bit right the rest would foll
natically. I thought of that first sentence as a kind of semantic womb stuf

D0536562

Firmin

Firmin

Adventures of a Metropolitan Lowlife

Sam Savage

Weidenfeld & Nicolson
LONDON

First published in Great Britain in 2008
by Weidenfeld & Nicolson

© Sam Savage 2006
First published by Coffee House Press, Minneapolis, Minnesota, USA
© 2007 Editorial Seix Barral, Av. Diagonal 662–664,08034 Barcelona

Illustrations © Fernando Krahn 2007

1 3 5 7 9 10 8 6 4 2

All rights reserved. No part of this publication may be reproduced, stored in a retrieval system, or transmitted, in any form or by any means, electronic, mechanical, photocopying, recording or otherwise, without the prior permission of both the copyright owner and the above publisher.

The right of Sam Savage to be identified as the author of this work has been asserted in accordance with the Copyright, Designs and Patents Act 1988.

A CIP catalogue record for this book
is available from the British Library

ISBN 978 0 297 85458 6 (hardback)

Typeset by Input Data Services Ltd,
Bridgwater, Somerset

Printed and bound in Great Britain by
Clays Ltd, St Ives plc

Weidenfeld & Nicolson
An imprint of the Orion Publishing Group
Orion House, 5 Upper St Martin's Lane,
London WC2H 9EA

www.orionbooks.co.uk

To Nora

One day Chuang Tzu fell asleep, and while he slept he dreamed that he was a butterfly, flying happily about. And this butterfly did not know that it was Chuang Tzu dreaming. Then he awoke, to all appearances himself again, but now he did not know whether he was a man dreaming that he was a butterfly or a butterfly dreaming he was a man.

—*The Teachings of Chuang Tzu*

Had he kept a pain diary, the only entry would have been one word: Myself.

—*Philip Roth*

Chapter 1

I had always imagined that my life story, if and when I wrote it, would have a great first line: something lyric like Nabokov's 'Lolita, light of my life, fire of my loins'; or if I could not do lyric, then something sweeping like Tolstoy's 'All happy families are alike, but every unhappy family is unhappy in its own way.' People remember those words even when they have forgotten everything else about the books. When it comes to openers, though, the best in my view has to be the beginning of Ford Madox Ford's *The Good Soldier*: 'This is the saddest story I have ever heard.' I've read that one dozens of times and it still knocks my socks off. Ford Madox Ford was a Big One.

In all my life struggling to write I have struggled with nothing so manfully – yes, that's the word, *manfully* – as with openers. It has always seemed to me that if I could just get that bit right all the rest would follow automatically. I thought of that first sentence as a kind of semantic womb stuffed with the busy embryos of unwritten pages, brilliant little nuggets of genius practically panting to be born. From that grand vessel the entire story would, so to speak, ooze forth. What a delusion! Exactly the opposite was true. And it is not as if there weren't any good ones. Savor this, for example:

'When the phone rang at 3:00 a.m. Morris Monk knew even before picking up the receiver that the call was from a dame, and he knew something else too: dames meant trouble.' Or this: 'Just before being hacked to pieces by Gamel's sadistic soldiers, Colonel Benchley had a vision of the little whitewashed cottage in Shropshire, and Mrs Benchley in the doorway, and the children.' Or this: 'Paris, London, Djibouti, all seemed unreal to him now as he sat amid the ruins of yet another Thanksgiving dinner with his mother and father and that idiot Charles.' Who can remain unimpressed by sentences like these? They are so pregnant with meaning, so, I dare say, poignant with it that they positively bulge with whole unwritten chapters – unwritten, but there, already there!

Alas, in reality they were nothing but bubbles, illusions every one. Each of the wonderful phrases, so full of promise, was like a gift-wrapped box clutched in a small child's eager hand, a box that holds nothing but gravel and bits of trash, though it rattles oh so enticingly. He thinks it is candy! I thought it was literature. All those sentences – and many, many others as well – proved to be not springboards to the great unwritten novel but insurmountable barriers to it. You see, they were too *good*. I could never live up to them. Some writers can never equal their first novel. I could never equal my first sentence. And look at me now. Look how I have begun this, my final work, my opus: 'I had always imagined that my life story, if and when ...' Good God, 'if and when'! You see the problem. Hopeless. Scratch it.

*

This is the saddest story I have ever heard. It begins, like all true stories, who knows where. Looking for the beginning is like trying to discover the source of a river. You paddle upstream for months under a burning sun, between towering green walls of dripping jungle, soggy maps disintegrating in your hands. You are driven half mad by false hopes, malicious swarms of biting insects, and the tricks of memory, and all you reach at the end – the ultima Thule of the whole ridiculous quest – is a damp spot in the jungle or, in the case of a story, some perfectly meaningless word or gesture. And yet, at some more or less arbitrary place along the way between the damp spot and the sea the cartographer inserts the point of his compass, and there the Amazon begins.

It is the same with me, cartographer of the soul, when I look for the beginning of my life story. I close my eyes and stab. I open them and discover a fluttering instant impaled on my compass point: 3:17 p.m. on the thirtieth of April, 1961. I scrunch up my eyes and bring it into focus. Moment, moment on a pin, where's the fellow with no chin? And there I am – or, rather, there I was – peering cautiously out over the edge of a balcony, just the tip of my nose and one eye. That balcony was a good spot for a looker, a sly peerer like me. From it I could survey the whole shop floor and yet not be seen by any of the people below. That day the store was crowded, more customers than usual for a weekday, and their murmurs floated pleasantly up. It was a beautiful spring afternoon, and some of these people had probably been out for a stroll, thinking about this and that, when their inattention was diverted by a large hand-painted sign in the store window: 30% OFF ALL PURCHASES OVER $20. But I wouldn't really know about that, I mean about what might have attracted them into the store, since I have had no actual experience with the exchange value of money. And indeed the balcony, the store, the customers, even the spring, require explanations, digressions that, however necessary, would wreck the pace of my narrative, which I like to think of as headlong. I have obviously gone too far – in my enthusiasm to get the whole thing going I have overshot the mark. We may never know where a story begins, but we sometimes can tell where it *cannot* begin, where the stream is already in full flood.

I close my eyes and stab again. I unfold the fluttering instant and pin its wings to the desk: 1:42 a.m., November 9, 1960. It was cold and damp in Boston's Scollay Square, and poor ignorant Flo – whom I would know shortly as Mama – had taken refuge in the basement of a shop on Cornhill. In her great fright she had somehow contrived to squeeze herself into the far end of a very narrow slot between a large metal cylinder and the concrete wall of the cellar, and she crouched there shaking with fear and cold. She could hear from up on the street level the shouts and laughter drifting away across the Square. They had almost had her that time – five men in sailor suits, stamping and kicking and shouting like crazy people. She had been zigzagging this way and that – fool them as to your intention, hope they crash into each other – when a polished black shoe caught her a blow to the ribs that sent her flying across the sidewalk.

So how did she escape?

The way we always escape. By a miracle: the darkness, the rain, a crack in a doorway, a misstep by a pursuer. *Pursuit and Escape in America's Oldest Cities*. In the scramble of her panic she had managed to get all the way around behind the curved metal thing, so that only a faint glow reached her from the lighted basement, and there she crouched a long time without moving. She closed her eyes against the pain in her side and focused her mind instead on the delicious warmth of the cellar that was rising slowly through her body like a tide. The metal thing was deliciously warm. Its enameled smoothness felt soft, and she pressed her trembling body up against it. Perhaps she slept. Yes, I am sure of it, she slept, and she woke refreshed.

And then, timid and uncertain, she must have crept from her cave out into the room. A faintly humming fluorescent lamp hanging by a pair of twisted wires from the ceiling cast a flickering bluish light on her surroundings. On *her* surroundings? What a laugh! On my surroundings! For all around her, everywhere she looked, were books. Floor to ceiling against every wall as well as against both sides of a counter-high partition that ran down the center of the room stood unpainted wooden shelves into which rows of books had been jammed to bursting. Other books, mostly taller volumes, had been wedged in flat on top of these, while still others rose in towering ziggurats from the floor or lay in precarious stacks and sloping piles on top of the partition. This warm musty place where she had found refuge was a mausoleum of books, a museum of forgotten treasures, a cemetery of the unread and unreadable. Old leatherbound tomes, cracked and mildewed, rubbed shoulders with cheap newer books whose yellowing pages had gone brown and brittle at the edges. There were Zane Grey westerns by the saddleload, books of lugubrious sermons by the casketful, old encyclopedias, memoirs of the Great War, diatribes against the New Deal, instruction manuals for the New Woman. But of course Flo did not know that these things were books. *Adventures on the Planet Earth. I* enjoy picturing her as she peers about at this strange landscape – her kind, worn face, her stout body, no, her rotund body, the glittering, hunted eyes, and the cute way she has of wrinkling her nose. Sometimes, just for fun, I put a little blue kerchief on her and knot it at the chin, and then *adorable* says it all. Mama!

High in one wall were two small windows. The panes were grimed black with soot and hard to see through, but she could make out that it was still night. She could also hear the quickening pace of the traffic in the street and knew from long habit that another workday was set to begin. The shop above would be opening, perhaps people would be coming down the steep wooden steps into the basement. People down the steps, maybe man-people, big feet, big shoes. *Thump*. She had to hurry, and – let's have this out now – not just because she was not keen on being caught by the sailors and kicked again or worse. She had to hurry especially because of the huge thing that was going on inside of her. Well, not a thing exactly, though there were indeed things inside of her (thirteen of them), more like a process, the sort of happening that people, with their enormous sense of humor, call a Blessed Event. A Blessed Event was about to occur, there was no question about it. The only question is, whose blessed event was it? Hers? Or mine? For most of my life I was convinced it had to have been anybody's but mine. But leaving me aside – oh, if only I could! – and returning to the situation in the basement: there was the Blessed Event on the verge of happening, and the question was what Flo (Mama) was going to do about it.

Well, I'll tell you what she did about it.

She went over to the shelf nearest the little cave in back of the warm metal thing and pulled down the biggest book she could get her paws on. She pulled it out and opened it, and holding a page down with her feet she tore it into confetti with her teeth. She did this with a second page, and a third. But here I detect a doubt. How, I hear you asking, do I know that she chose the *biggest* book? Well, as Jeeves likes to say, it is a question of the psychology of the individual, who in this case is Flo, my impending mother. 'Rotund' was, I fear, too kind. She was disgustingly overweight, and just the daily grind of stoking all that fat had made her horribly edgy. Edgy and piggy. Urged on by the voracious clamor of millions of starving cells, she was always sure to grab the biggest slice of anything, even if she was already stuffed to the gills and could only nibble at the edges. Spoiled it for everyone else, of course. So rest assured, the biggest volume around is the one she went for.

Sometimes I like to think that the first moments of my struggle toward existence were accompanied, as by a triumphal march, by the shredding of *Moby-Dick*. That would account for the extreme adventurousness of my nature. At other times, when I am feeling particularly outcast and freakish, I am convinced that *Don Quixote* is the culprit. Just listen to this: 'In short, he so immersed himself in those romances that he spent whole days and nights over his books; and thus with little sleeping and much reading, his brains dried up to such a degree that he lost the use of his reason. Having lost his wits completely, he stumbled upon the oddest fancy that had ever entered a madman's brain. He believed that it was necessary, both for his own honor and the service of the state, that he should become a knight-errant.' Behold the Knight of Rueful Figure: fatuous, pigheaded, clownish, naive to the point of blindness, idealistic to the point of grotesqueness – and who is that if not me in a nutshell? The truth is, I have never been right in the head. Only I don't charge windmills. I do worse: I *dream* of charging windmills, I *long* to charge windmills, and sometimes even I *imagine* I have charged windmills. Windmills or the mills of culture or – let's say it – those most delectable of all unconquerable objects, those erotic grinders, lascivious little mills of lust, carnal factories of kinky joys,

fantasylands of frustrated fornicators, my Lovelies' own bodies. And what difference does it make in the end? A hopeless cause is a hopeless cause. But I won't obsess about that now. I'll obsess about it later.

Mama had made a huge pile of paper and with great effort was dragging and shoving it back into that little dark cavern she had found. And here we must not allow ourselves to become so distracted by the doleful cacophony of her portly grunts and wheezes as to lose sight of the fundamental question: where did all that paper come from? Whose broken words and shattered sentences did Mama churn into the indecipherable mélange that, moments later, would cushion my fall into existence? I am straining my eyes to see. It is very dark in that place where she has pushed the pile and where now she is busy stamping it down in the middle and humping it up at the edges, and I can see it clearly only by leaning over the precipice that is the moment I was born. I am looking down at it from a great height, screwing up my imagination into a kind of telescope. I think I see it. Yes, I recognize it now. Dear Flo has made confetti of *Finnegans Wake*. Joyce was a Big One, maybe the Biggest One. I was birthed, bedded, and suckled on the defoliated carcass of the world's most unread masterpiece.

Mine was a large family, and soon thirteen of us were cruddled in its struins, to speak like itself, 'chippy young cuppinjars cluttering round, clottering for their creams.' (And after all these years, here I am hard at it still – clottering, dottering, for my creams, my crumbs. O dreams!) All of us were soon fighting it out over twelve tits: Sweeny, Chucky, Luweena, Feenie, Mutt, Peewee, Shunt, Pudding, Elvis, Elvina, Humphrey, Honeychild, and Firmin (that's me, the thirteenth child). I remember them all so well. They were monsters. Even blind and naked, especially naked, their limbs bulged with sinew and muscle, or so it seemed to me at the time. I alone was born with my eyes wide open and clothed in a modest coat of soft gray fur. I was also puny. And take it from me, being puny is a terrible thing when you are little.

It had an especially damaging effect on my ability to participate fully in the feeding routine, which usually went something like this: Mama tumbles home to the basement from wherever it is she has been, in her customary foul mood. Grunting and complaining as if she were about to do something so heroic that no other mother in the history of the world had ever even thought of doing it, she flops down on the bed – *kerplop* – and falls instantly asleep, gape-mouthed and snoring and totally deaf to the chaos breaking out around her. Clawing, shoving, biting, squealing, all thirteen of us simultaneously dive for the twelve nipples. *Milk and Madness*. In this game of musical tits, I was almost always the one left standing. Sometimes I think of myself as He Who Was Left Standing. I have found that putting it that way helps. And even when I did occasionally manage to be first man on, I was soon muscled off by one of my more sinewy siblings. It's a miracle that I made it out of my family alive. As it was, I survived pretty much on leftovers. Even today, just by remembering, I can feel

again that awful sliding sensation as the nipple slips from my mouth, as I am dragged backward by my hind feet. People talk about despair as a hollow feeling in the gut or a coldness or a nausea, but to me it will always be that slipping-away feeling in my mouth and across my gums.

But what do I hear now? Is it silence, an *embarrassed* silence? You are pulling at your chin and thinking, 'Well, *that* explains everything. This character has spent his whole useless life just searching for the thirteenth tit.' And what can I say? Should I grovel and admit it? Or should I protest and cry out, 'Is that *all*? Is that really *all*?'

Chapter 2

Every night Mama left us to sneak out to the Square, to go 'up top,' as we called it, for supplies. The neighborhood was a good place for foraging in those days. After the bars and strip joints had shut down for the night most people liked to throw things on the sidewalks. Along with the paper bags, crushed beer cans, cigarette packs, and vomit, they also threw plenty of nutritious stuff, sometimes whole untouched meals. In addition, the City of Boston was cracking down on lowlifes, which in those days included pretty much the entire population of the neighborhood, and had stopped picking up garbage to punish them. The gutters overflowed with provender, and people had to watch where they stepped.

Mama would be gone for what seemed like forever, and we would horse around there in the dark, even though we were supposed to be very quiet on account of not being legal tenants. We were in fact squatters, though seeing that the whole kit and caboodle, the bookshop, the strip joints, even the garbage cans, were on a straight path to oblivion, with us just hanging on for the ride, maybe *stowaways* would be more accurate. But we didn't know that yet, I mean about the ride to oblivion. At that age you think everything is forever.

After what seemed hours and hours, when we were practically desperate with hunger, we would hear her coming back. *We* were supposed to be very quiet, and there would come Mama crashing and stumbling down the stairs.

I may as well call a spade a spade and say right off that Mama was some kind of tosspot. That – and her enormous girth – accounted for her problems with the stairs. In those days you could lap up booze off the sidewalks in our neighborhood, and Flo was not one to lay obstacles in the path of temptation. She was that kind of girl; it was that kind of neighborhood. So she was always pretty well tanked when she finally tumbled back home, which probably explains how she could nod off in the midst of all that shoving and squealing. Out like a light and snoring, that was Mama. A lot of people have boozehounds for parents, nothing special in that, but looking back I can see that in my case it was a great piece of luck and probably saved my life. *Alcoholism's Silver Lining: A Child's Story*. By the time she tottered back from one of those trips up top she usually had soaked up so much sauce her milk would set your head spinning. Not mine, of course. I was predictably off on the sidelines somewhere eating my heart out while the rest of them slurped and gurgled the great-tasting stuff she had brought home, stuff that would have caught fire had there been a spark. In the end, however, alcoholic beverage had the same effect on my brothers and sisters as it had on Mama, and one by one they nodded off, the nipples slipping from their little pink-gummed mouths. By this time, of course, most of the alcohol had worked its way out of Flo's system and the milk was starting to run pure. So all I had to do was clamber over the rows of sleepy little tipplers and go from tit to tit emptying the last delicious drops from each. It was never enough. But it made the difference, keeping me alive, though just barely.

I don't have to lean out over the precipice of my birth to find Mama anymore. Now I could lie on my back in the confetti, adorable pink feet curling in the air above me, and look up at her great bulk. And I did this often. Yet the picture of Mama I have kept from that moment, aside from the sheer mass of her, is scarcely more than a featureless blur. I scrunch up my eyes, I drag out my telescope, I focus, I focus – and I hardly see anything. When I think of Mama at this point nothing enters my mind but *words.* I screw my concentration up to the point where I am almost fainting, and still nothing is there but a blurred shape and the words *not enough tits* – that, and a thick sawdust-and-beer fragrance like a saloon floor.

I have not been able to get around much in the so-called real world, but I have done a lot of traveling in my head, riding my thoughts this way and that. Once on one of these trips I met a man in a bar who told me a story about when he was a small boy in Berlin, Germany, right at the end of the war. That would be the Second World War. The whole city had just been bombed to smithereens, so it looked a lot like Scollay Square is going to look a little later in this story, and it

was winter and cold and there was nothing to eat. His house, what was left of it, was very dark and cold, so this little boy spent most of his time sitting on the sidewalk in the shelter of a sunlit wall where it was a little warmer. He sat there for hours every day and dreamed about food. The street in front of his house had a big hole in it where a bomb had fallen. People had partially filled it in, but it was still a hole, and one day a truck loaded with coal came rolling down the street. The driver didn't see the crater in time and the truck hit it, *kerbang*. There was a tremendous jolt and a lot of coal fell off the truck. But the truck did not stop. It went on around the turn, and for a moment there was just this empty sunlit street littered with coal. One small piece had rolled over right next to the little boy's foot. And then all of a sudden, as if on cue, doors flew open up and down the street, and men and women, mostly women, came rushing out. The little boy looked on in amazement as they started snatching up the pieces of coal, gathering them in their aprons and baskets and even fighting over them. He put his foot on top of the little piece that lay on the ground beside him, and later, when the people had all gone back inside, he slipped it into his pocket. From the behavior of the women he could tell it was something very valuable, though he had no idea what it was. Then he went around the corner and took it out of his pocket and tried to eat it.

And in Africa during famines the starving children eat dirt. If you are hungry enough, you will eat anything. Just the act of chewing and swallowing something, even if it does not nourish the body, nourishes your dreams. And dreams of food are just like other dreams – you can live on them till you die.

In the basement of the bookshop where we lived there was not any coal and there was not any real dirt. There was plenty of dust, but you can't eat dust. It sticks to the roof of your mouth and is impossible to swallow. Paper, on the other hand, I discovered early on, has a wonderful consistency and in some cases an agreeable taste. You can masticate a hunk of it for hours if you want, like gum. Shoved off to the side by my muscular siblings, biding my time while trying to fill the gnawing hollow in my gut with vast imaginary repasts, I started chewing on the confetti at my feet.

Despite the fact that I was barely out of my infancy, I think it fair to call this moment the beginning of the end for me. Like many things that start as small, illicit pleasures, paper chewing soon became a habit, with its own imperative, and then an addiction, a mortal hunger whose satisfaction was so delightful that I would often hesitate to pounce on the first free tit. I would instead stand there chewing until the wad in my mouth had softened to a delectable paste that I could mash against the roof of my mouth or mold into interesting shapes with my tongue and safely swallow. Unfortunately, the chewed paper left a sticky coating on my mouth and tongue that lasted for hours and caused me to smack my lips in a truly unpleasant manner.

I started slowly, with a nibble here and

there, but in next to no time I was on a roll, and in just a few days I had managed to tuck away so much of the communal bed that patches of bare concrete were showing through. This caused no end of bad feelings between me and the others and even earned me a few sharp drubbings, but I did not let that stop me. I can be very determined when I put my mind to it.

In the end, to stop the bickering, Mama had to go out and drag back a few more pages of the Great Book. We were getting pretty big now, so we all joined in the shredding party. Squeaking with delight, we ripped and tore with a vengeance. There is nothing like destruction for creating a warm sense of camaraderie, and for a few minutes there in the rough-and-tumble of it all we actually felt like a big happy family. When people ask me to recount something from my childhood, I always trot that one out, just to show that we were normal.

Needless to say, the arrival of all this fresh paper that no one had ever shat or pissed on did nothing to tame my appetite, and I must have put away whole chapters by the time I was old enough to toddle on wobbly fours out of our dark corner and into the flickering bigness. I am convinced that these masticated pages furnished the nutritional foundation for – and perhaps even directly caused – what I with modesty shall call my unusual mental development. Imagine: the history of the world in four parts, fragments of philosophy, psychoanalysis, linguistics, astronomy, astrology, hundreds of rivers, popular songs, the Bible, the Koran, the Bhagavad Gita, the Book of the Dead, the French

Revolution, the Russian Revolution, hundreds of insects, street signs, advertisements, Kant, Hegel, Swedenborg, comic strips, nursery rhymes, London and Thessalonica, Sodom and Gomorrah, the history of literature, the history of Ireland, accusations of unspeakable crimes, confessions, denials, thousands of puns, dozens of languages, recipes, dirty jokes, illnesses, childbirths, executions – all this and more I took into my body. Took it in, I admit, before I was ready. I have a vivid, even visceral, recollection of my young self curled up in a dark corner on a bed of shredded paper (my future meals), clutching a grotesquely distended abdomen and groaning with pain. Oh, such pain! – the long crescendoing cramps burrowing and twisting as they gnawed their way through my shuddering bowels. I still find it amazing that this repeated agony did not put me off paper chewing forever. But of course it did not. I had only to wait for the pain to pass before beginning anew, and sometimes I could not wait even that long.

Do I hear snickering? I suppose you see this as merely a rather vulgar case of addiction or perhaps as the pitiable symptoms of a classic obsessive-compulsive disorder, and no doubt you are correct. Yet the concept of addiction is not rich enough, *deep* enough, to describe this hunger. I would rather call it *love*. Inchoate perhaps, perverted even, unrequited surely, but love all same. Here was the crude glutinous beginning of the passion that has dominated my life, some would say ruined it, and I would not necessarily disagree. Had I been more astute I might have been able to see the dreadful abdominal pain that followed the exercise of this passion in its infantile form as a warning, an augury of the interminable sufferings that seem always to accompany love.

Eaten daily – or in my case almost constantly, if one includes the subsequent smacking at the sticky after-coating – even the most delectable dish eventually cloys. I am ashamed to say it, but as time went on the Great Book slid ineluctably down the scale of charms toward insipidity, grew increasingly tasteless, boring, scarcely more than cardboard really. I needed a change of diet. And besides, I had grown weary of drubbings.

So one day I decided to give my family a break and carry my chewings out into the stacks. It was Sunday morning the first time I ventured out. The shop above was closed, and there was almost no traffic in the Square to add its distant harmony to the blended snores of my stupefied family. Slipping down the passageway that led from our homey corner and out into the flickering big room, nose to the floor, the first thing I came across, sprawled open on the cement, was the Great Book itself, or what was left of it. I recognized it instantly by its smell. Inhaled in this concentrated, multifoliate form, hundreds of pages packed densely together, it made me a little queasy. *The Impact of Genius*. I looked up at the remaining books in the low shelf from which Mama had dragged this one and found that I could make out the titles quite easily. Obviously even at that early age I was already suffering from the catastrophic gift of lexical hypertrophy, which has since done so much to mar the smooth course of what might otherwise have been a perfectly ordinary life. Above this group of shelves was a handwritten paper sign bearing the word FICTION and a crude blue arrow pointing straight downward. As I explored the room further in the days and weeks that followed I came across other signs saying HISTORY, RELIGION, PSYCHOLOGY, SCIENCE, BARGAINS, and RESTROOM.

I regard this period as the decisive beginning of my education, even though the craving that was driving me out from my cozy corner and into the big world was not yet a hunger for knowledge. I began with the closest shelves, the ones under FICTION, licking, nibbling, savoring, and finally eating, sometimes around the edges, but usually, whenever I could pry the covers open, straight through the middle like a drill. My favorites were the Modern Library editions, and I always chose one of those when I could, perhaps because of their logo – a runner with a torch. At times I have thought of myself as a Runner with a Torch. And oh, what books I discovered during those first intoxicating days! Even today the mere recitation of the titles brings tears to my eyes. Recite them, then, say them slowly aloud and let them break your heart. *Oliver Twist. Huckleberry Finn. The Great Gatsby. Dead Souls. Middlemarch. Alice in Wonderland. Fathers and Sons. The Grapes of Wrath. The Way of All Flesh. An American Tragedy. Peter Pan. The Red and the Black. Lady Chatterley's Lover.*

My devourings at first were crude, orgiastic,

unfocused, piggy – a mouthful of Faulkner was a mouthful of Flaubert as far as I was concerned – though I soon began to notice subtle differences. I noticed first that each book had a different flavor – sweet, bitter, sour, bittersweet, rancid, salty, tart. I also noticed that each flavor – and, as time passed and my senses grew more acute, the flavor of each page, each sentence, and finally each word – brought with it an array of images, representations in the mind of things I knew nothing about from my very limited experiences in the so-called real world: skyscrapers, harbors, horses, cannibals, a flowering tree, an unmade bed, a drowned woman, a flying boy, a severed head, field hands looking up at the sound of an idiot howling, a train whistle, a river, a raft, sun slanting through a forest of birches, a hand caressing a naked thigh, a jungle hut, a dying monk.

At first I just ate, happily gnawing and chewing, guided by the dictates of taste. But soon I began to read here and there around the edges of my meals. And as time passed I read more and chewed less until finally I was spending almost all my waking hours reading and chewed only on the margins. And oh, how I then regretted those dreadful holes! In some cases, where there were no other copies, I have had to wait years to fill the gaps. I am not proud of this.

Now, buffeted and stunned by life, I look back at my childhood in the hope of finding there some confirmation of my worth, some sign that I was destined at least for a time to be something other than a dilettante and a buffoon, that I was defeated by inexorable

circumstance and not by a flaw within. Let them say, 'Hard luck, Firmin,' and not, 'We could have told you so.' I scrunch up my eyes and point my telescope, but, alas, it picks out no divine afflatus, magnifies not even a few sparks of genius, discovers nothing but an eating disorder. Instead of telescopes, the doctors will haul out their stethoscopes, their electroencephalograms, their polygraphs, all in support of the crushing diagnosis: a routine case of biblio-bulimia. And the worst of it is, *they will be right*. And in the face of this essential rightness, the demeaning obviousness of their crushing judgment – *crushing* is a word I like using – I want to cry out at myself like old Ezra Pound locked in his rat's cage in Pisa, 'Pull down thy vanity, I say pull down.' Pound was a Big One.

But enough of this. The small creature I was back then had as yet no inkling of such agonies. Back then, perched on the lowest rung of the ladder of life, I was still the Sabbath child, bonny and blithe, and those were happy days in the bookshop. Or, I should say, happy nights and Sundays, since I did not dare venture out into that flickering vastness during the hours when people were in the store. From our dim basement covert we could hear the murmur of voices and the creak of footsteps on the ceiling. Hear them and tremble. Sometimes the footsteps would leave the ceiling and come down the wooden stairs into the basement. Usually this descent was followed by a period of silence, but sometimes it would be followed by gruntings and growlings, even inexplicable explosions, and these frightened us terribly. After that would come the noise of rushing water, and then footsteps on the stairs again. The footsteps going up were never as loud as the ones coming down.

Chapter 3

One night while I was poking around under BARGAINS, I noticed a crude hole in the masonry where a large black pipe came out of the wall. It snaked across the floor and slithered into the opposite wall under RESTROOM. There were no shelves against that wall, just a door, and that was always closed. I poked my nose into the hole and sniffed. It smelled of rats. The pipe entered the wall and then turned and ran straight up. Though it was a very big pipe, it did not entirely fill the hole that had been made for it, and the masonry all around it was rough and jagged. I had a lot of curiosity in those days, and the smell was reassuring, though it was not exactly like the rat smells I was used to. It was sadder than those.

Bracing my back against the pipe, I placed my feet against the side of the hole and hauled myself up using the jagged bits of masonry as toeholds. It was a fairly easy climb. At the top, at a level corresponding to the baseboards on the first floor, the tunnel branched. One path went on up along the pipe, while others snaked left and right along the base of the wall between the plaster laths and the exterior masonry. That night I went left. The next night I went right. And in a week I had a map of the whole system in my head. The building was veined with tunnels, a regular honeycomb, a twisting, back-looping warren. If I were not in such a hurry – there is almost no more time – I could at this point launch into an interminable description of the whole tunnel system, which obviously had been constructed by the cooperative labor of thousands of rats long before my time, generations of them grinding their incisors to stubs just so I, Firmin, could one day travel undetected to every point in the building. I could break your ears talking about shafts, chutes, scopes, and drifts, about the difference between a raise and a winze, and if anybody was still awake I could put him to sleep with glory holes, scrapers, dippers, manladders, and footwalls. If you enjoy that sort of description, you should get a book on mining.

At first I expected to bump into other rats at every turn, the builders of this cavernous city, but I never did. I eventually came to think of them as 'erstwhile.' I never found any food either. And maybe that is why there were no more rats. Before the shop became a bookstore, perhaps it had been a grocery store or a bakery. Now there was nothing to eat but paper. Yet my patient exploration, night after night, of what seemed like miles of tunnel finally brought rewards that were to me superior to any food. You have to keep in mind that these intramural shafts were totally dark. I have excellent night vision, but there I had to feel my way by smell and touch. It was slow, tedious work, and it was several days before I stumbled upon a chute that took me directly up into the ceiling over the main room of the shop. The building, like most buildings in that part of town, was very old, without insulation in the ceiling, and the space between each pair of joists formed a long open chamber, incredibly hot and dusty. My dogged forebears had gnawed neat circular holes in the joists, and by means of these holes I was able to clamber from chamber to chamber. I was working my way in the direction of the street, exploring each chamber thoroughly with feet and nose before moving on to the next, when I came upon something so unexpected it set me back on my heels. After more than a week of nights spent groping in inky blackness, here suddenly were rays of light streaming up through the floor from the shop below. At some point long ago someone – not a rat – had cut a large round hole in the shop ceiling for a light fixture, which had then been installed slightly off center, leaving a narrow crescent-shaped opening along its rim. Peering cautiously through this crack I looked down into the room below.

Directly beneath me stood a large cluttered desk and a chair with a red cushion. This desk and chair were where Norman sat, or would sit. I still did not know Norman – for some time yet he was to sit in my mind simply as the Owner of the Desk – but the clutter on the desk, the upright steel spike stacked to its tip with a ragged foliage of impaled receipts, the shiny arms of the chair, and of course the red cushion itself with its buttocks-shaped depression in the center, possessed an aura of seriousness and dignity that, considering my background, I found perfectly irresistible.

This ceiling crack, shaped like a C for Confidential, became one of my favorite spots. It was a window on the human world, my first window. In that way it was like a book – you could look through it into worlds that were not your own. I called it the Balloon, because that was the feeling I got looking down, as if I were floating above the room in a balloon. A few days later I discovered a second very good place all the way at the other end of the ceiling in the direction of the alley. This one was a jagged hole in the plaster where a makeshift partition met the ceiling. I could lower myself through this hole and down onto the top of one of the tall glass-fronted cabinets where Norman kept the rare books, and from there I commanded a magnificent view of the main room of the shop, including the front door and Norman's desk and chair. I named it the Balcony. (Today the words *balcony* and *balloon*, dactyl and iamb, have become fused end to end to form a kind of cradle, or a sad little boat. Sometimes I climb in the boat and float around. Or I lie in the cradle and rock and suck my toe.) I later learned that this room, which at the time seemed to me practically oceanic in its vastness, was in fact only one small piece of the operation. Norman had room upon room. At some point long before my time he had acquired the two shops next door to the original bookstore and had knocked holes in the connecting walls. Passing through narrow doorways, so narrow people had to take turns going through or else walk sideways and rub stomachs, you entered the rooms one after another, and they were full of books too. I used to think that all those rooms connected by little doorways were like something a giant rat would build, and I enjoyed that thought once, before Norman let me down.

Sometimes the books were arranged under signs, but sometimes they were just anywhere and everywhere. After I understood people better, I realized that this incredible disorder was one of the things that they loved about Pembroke Books. They did not come there just to buy a book, plunk down some cash and scram. They hung around. They called it browsing, but it was more like excavation or mining. I was surprised they didn't come in with shovels. They dug for treasures with bare hands, up to their armpits sometimes, and when they hauled some literary nugget from a mound of dross, they were much happier than if they had just walked in and bought it. In that way shopping at Pembroke was like reading: you never knew what you might encounter on the next page – the next shelf, stack, or box – and that was part of the pleasure of it. And that was part of the pleasure of the tunnels too – you could never be sure what was around the next turn, at the bottom of the next shaft.

Even during those first heady weeks of exploration, I did not neglect my education. I never went into the tunnels without first spending a few hours with my books. And I made tremendous progress. I was soon able to comprehend even so-called difficult novels, mostly Russian and French, and was making headway in simple works of philosophy and business administration. It is clear to me now, from my subsequent researches, that such accomplishments were possible,

organically speaking, only on the basis of a steady growth in my frontal and temporal lobes, accompanied, I surmise, by a tremendous swelling of the angular gyrus. Reasoning backward from effect to cause, I feel justified in assuming that my cranium also conceals beneath its humdrum exterior an exceptional lateral elongation of Wernicke's area, a deformation that is normally associated with precocious verbal skills, though it is also, I concede, present in certain rare forms of idiocy. I attribute this unusual growth to a stimulating environment, though no doubt diet was a factor as well. It had, however, an unfortunate side effect in that my head grew so heavy I had difficulty holding it up. The cerebral muscularity, you see, was not accompanied by a corresponding corporal robustness. I was still distressingly runty. I was a pip-squeak, a shrimp.

It is practically an axiom in psychiatry that precocious intellect combined with physical weakness can give rise to many unpleasant character traits – avarice, delusions of grandeur, and obsessive masturbation, to name just a few. And indeed it is because certain so-called experts possess, via the most rudimentary handbooks, such a ready-made insight into the very depths of my character that all my life I have taken pains to avoid them – I am referring to psychiatrists. This aversion is only natural, I think, when you consider that among other lamentable effects occasioned by my condition one invariably finds a near-pathological need to hide or, that failing, to wear masks.

The combination of a heavy head and weak limbs

forced me to adopt a ponderous gait, and while later in life I fancied that this lent me a methodical and dignified air, at the time it only made me seem all the more freakish. I could not help wagging my enormous head from side to side as I walked, or lumbered, which gave me a rather bovine appearance. And front-loaded as I was, I had a strong tendency to pitch forward onto my face, to the great amusement of others.

Such ponderousness, so grotesque in a creature of my stature, was particularly unfortunate at this period, when I had reached a stage of life that called for maximum alacrity. While nothing in the behavior of my siblings suggested that their brains were expanding, their masticatory apparatuses had undergone considerable development, as I could testify from many painful nips. I chewed on paper, they chewed on me. The asymmetry was nasty. All of us were ready for solid food. We were all in fact ready to throw in the towel on family life, and Mama discerned this through her vapors at last. Our flashing incisors must have seemed to her like glimmers of light at the end of the long maternal tunnel. Lured by that light she rose to the task of teaching us to get by without her, setting us up so she could split and go off and lead the life of a swinger again.

Our education was simple and practical. Two by two we tagged along behind Mama on her trips up top, where we were expected to learn by observing her technique. There was not going to be any more easy slurp and guzzle: from now on we would confront an entirely new style of existence. Anthropologists regard hunting and gathering as the most primitive stage of civilization, but ours was even lower than that. Call it scrounging and scraping. It was almost entirely night work. The basic positions were crouch, skulk, and hunker. The sustaining moves were creep, scurry, and dart. When my turn came I was paired with Luweena. I was pleased with this, since she had always treated me with indifference, offering me neither nips nor drubs, which was all to the good, since she was of large athletic build and once during a melee had bitten off most of Shunt's ear. I had always been aware – and wary – of her build, but that night, just as we were starting out, I noticed for the first time how furry she was behind. It was not only her teeth that were growing. Preoccupied as I was with my explorations, I had let this new development slip up on me, but now the view of her furry cheeks bobbing in front of me became utterly distracting, and I felt toward her a sudden violent anger.

With Mama in the lead we crept under the cellar door and out into the world. I had thought of myself as being better prepared than any of the others for what we would encounter outside. It was I after all who had spent many hours sitting in my Balcony gazing out across the shop toward the front window. I had seen something of the world in that window – people and cars passing and part of the building across the street. Once I saw a policeman on a horse, and once it rained. But stepping out into the night street behind Luweena and Mama I knew right away that my picture of the world, limited and rectangular as it was, bore scarcely any resemblance to the enormity of the thing itself. I felt like an earthling stepping out onto the surface of Jupiter. We stepped out onto a hard black desert. The streetlight directly above us hung like a sun in a black sky. From somewhere, perhaps the streetlight, came a faint high-pitched scream that was painful to the ears and in the long run maddening in its persistence. On both sides, crumbling four-story buildings loomed like the walls of a vast canyon. Even at that early stage of my education I had read enough to formulate 'vast canyon of loneliness.' I formulated it and shivered. Now and then a car passed with blazing eyes, and the floor of the desert shook. It was very cold, and something like an icy comb was running through our fur. It was wind. Luweena, of course, with her more limited background, ought to have been even more amazed than I was. I would have expected her to cringe or at least gape in wonder or be in some way flabbergasted, and I was shocked to see her just sniff the air and trot off after Mama as though she regarded walking on Jupiter as a perfectly normal thing to do. As for me, I was still sheltered by my relative ignorance, and only a vague disquiet gnawed at the margins of my mind.

We went in single file, moving fast and staying as close to the buildings as we could, up Cornhill and then down a narrow alley. I brought up the rear. The alley was dark and had the same smell as under RESTROOM, but stronger. There must have been some kind of food there, for I could hear Mama and Luweena crunching on something in the darkness up ahead. They didn't share, and when I came up all I found was

a piece of lettuce. It tasted like *Jane Eyre*. We came out of the alley on Hanover Street, directly across from the bright blaze of the Casino Theater. On a jutting marquee, in yellow lights that ran round and round, were the words GIRLS, GIRLS, GIRLS and BEST IN BOSTON. Beneath the marquee, on either side of a glass ticket window, were life-sized black-and-white photos of what I have since learned to identify as good-looking women. They were not wearing any clothes except for high-heeled shoes and diamond tiaras in their hair, while two long black rectangles blocked out their breasts and the tops of their thighs. One woman had light hair and one had dark hair. They each had one foot lifted. Caught by the camera in the midst of dancing, they floated frozen in midstep: the stroke of the shutter had severed them from time like a guillotine. Mama and Luweena had paid them no attention at all. They had gone instead right up to the theater door under EXIT and were now busy stuffing their cheeks full of the popcorn someone had spilled there. Luweena clearly had a natural gift for scrounging and scraping. I did not even try to join them this time. I just stood there looking up at the posters, one foot in the air. Despite my wide reading, even my digestion of *Lady Chatterley's Lover*, I had only a pale intellectual's grasp of this aspect of the world. I had not actually *experienced* anything like it before. Now, looking back over my life, I can see that this moment, when I stood gaping at those almost naked creatures, those angels, marked what biographers like to call a turning point.
I shall do the same and say that on November

26, 1960, in front of the Casino Theater on a side street off Boston's Scollay Square, my life path turned. But of course I did not know that yet. At that point I did not even know I was in Boston.

Luweena and Mama having scooped up all the popcorn, we went on down Hanover, sliding along the gutter to the nearly deserted Square. The Square was, as people liked to say, a cesspool, and indeed the damp asphalt glistened under the streetlights like water. A woman, followed closely by a man, passed without seeing us. Walking rapidly, they turned and disappeared into a doorway under ROOMS. I shall never forget the sound the woman's heels made against the sidewalk. We crouched in a drain till they had gone inside, the door closed behind them. Then, following Mama's lead, we raced across the broad expanse of the Square as fast as we could go, as fast at any rate as Mama could go. In those days Luweena and I were still light on our feet. Reaching the opposite sidewalk, Mama found a puddle of beer, and she and Luweena refused to go on until they had lapped up every drop of it. My anxiety had by then migrated from the margins of my consciousness to dead center and I was beginning to quiver with fear. I thought, To hell with food. I wanted to run back home to the warm safety of the bookstore, but I was terrified of being separated from Mama. I was especially frightened by the trucks that now and then went thundering past us, their headlights throwing enormous shadows against the walls, though Mama did not even look up, and after a while neither did Luweena. And then we went on down the street. We passed in front of the darkened gothic-windowed hulk of the Old Howard, which had once been a famous theater but had been closed for years. A lot of low-class rats lived there. It was, Mama said, a good place to get killed. In the end, after more lapping and licking at sidewalk puddles, we found food – hot dogs, pickles, buns, ketchup, mustard – in the big blue bins in back of Joe and Nemo's. Other rats were there too but we stayed away from them. We are not a close-knit species. Then it was back out by the Red Hat Bar, and more puddles. Most of these were urine, but there were enough booze pools as well to keep Mama busy, and Luweena too. Bad genes, I guess. And the two of them grew increasingly reckless on the way home, at times walking in the middle of the sidewalk on Cambridge Street and singing. Not me, though. I skulked along right next to the buildings or in the gutter and pretended I didn't know them. In fact I kept my distance in the hope that if some huge calamity fell out of the sky on their heads it would miss me.

I am trying to tell the true story of my life, and believe me, it is not easy. I had read a great many of the books under FICTION before I halfway understood what that sign meant and why certain books had been placed under it. I had thought I was reading the history of the world. Even today I must constantly remind myself, sometimes by means of a rap on the head, that Eisenhower is real while Oliver Twist is not. *Lost in the World: Epistemology and Terror.* Thinking back on my account of that first sortie with Mama and Luweena out into the wilderness beyond our basement, I see

that I have left one small incident out. It was a perfectly trivial incident in my view but one that, were it discovered later, you would throw invidiously back in my face. I can already see you, swiveling around in your swivel chair and shrieking with delight. And besides, it was not an incident exactly, it was more like an incitement, or rather an attempt at incitement, by Luweena's furry behind.

While I was following her down the alley, it went, as I mentioned, up and down in front of my nose. Up and down. And the ridiculous thing was, she insisted on carrying her tail at a stimulating angle as well, an angle that I can fairly describe as brazen. Brazen and provocative. As we crept in single file down the alley, her behind filled my whole field of vision, invaded my consciousness and prevented me from thinking of anything else, even food and danger. And then of course there was the odor. I don't suppose I can make you understand that aspect of the thing, the irresistible power of that fragrance. It drove me to within an inch of leaping upon her like a madman. I felt myself being thrust forward by my groin. I saw myself leaping upon her from behind and sinking my incisors into the fur of her neck, while she curved her long muscular back, lifted her ass in the air, and with a squeak of delicious agony gave herself to me. It was horrible. But it was also mercifully brief. We were near the end of the alley already, approaching the lights of Hanover Street. A truck rumbled past and my sudden passion, strong as it was, vanished like smoke in its thunder. Nothing had happened. And nothing would happen, since at that moment we were already only yards and minutes from the turning point when I was to stand on the sidewalk, one foot lifted, and look up at the angels. Let me open my heart: that urge to ravish my sister in an alley was the last moment of normal sexual desire I ever experienced. When I set out that night I was, despite my intelligence, a fairly ordinary male. When I returned I was well on my way to becoming a pervert and a freak.

Chapter 4

In the world outside my beloved bookshop it was dog eat dog and devil take the hindmost. Everything out there was determined to do us mortal harm, always. Our one-year survival chances were close to zero. In fact, statistically speaking we were practically dead. I did not know this for a fact yet, but I had an intuition all the same, the kind of awful inkling people get on the decks of sinking ships. If there is one thing a literary education is good for it is to fill you with a sense of doom. There is nothing quite like a vivid imagination for sapping a person's courage. I read the diary of Anne Frank, I became Anne Frank. As for the others, they could feel plenty of terror, cringe in corners, sweat with fear, but as soon as the danger had passed it was as if it had never happened, and they trotted cheerfully on. Cheerfully on through life till they were flattened or poisoned or had their necks cracked by an iron bar. As for me, I have outlived them all and in exchange I have died a thousand deaths. I have moved through life trailing a glistening film of fear like a snail. When I actually die it will be an anticlimax.

One night not long after our orientation trip around the Square, Mama went up top as usual, and she never came back. I saw her a couple of times over the next few months hanging out with the floozies in back of Joe and Nemo's; then she vanished altogether. And that was the end of our little family. Every night after that somebody else went missing until finally only Luweena, Shunt, and I remained. And then they left too. They had trouble believing that I meant to stay on. To them I was mad, but harmless. They did not at all approve of what I was doing. The bookstore was after all a lousy place to live, and Mama had only chosen it in an emergency. Despite our past differences, the last day was almost touching. Luweena gave me a hug, and Shunt, embarrassed, handed me a little punch on the shoulder. They were disappearing beneath the door when I called after them, 'So long, you bunch of cocksuckers, you subhuman jerks.' I really told them off, and after that I felt better.

I moved into a little place I had arranged in the ceiling above the shop, midway between the Balloon and the Balcony, where I could keep track of things, while I continued my education at night in the basement, devouring book after book, though no longer literally. Well, that's not entirely true. Dwelling as I did each night in the mysterious interstices between reading and snacking, I had discovered a remarkable relation, a kind of preestablished harmony, between the taste and the literary quality of a book. To know if something was worth reading I had only to nibble a portion of the printed area. I learned to use the title page for this, leaving the text intact. 'Good to eat is good to read' became my motto.

Sometimes, to give my burning eyes a rest, I would go spelunking in the erstwhile ancestors' old shafts and secret rooms, and there one night, while creeping along behind the baseboard, I ran up against a dam of fallen plaster, a barrier I had previously mistaken for a portion of a wall but now saw was in fact a blocked tunnel. The obstructing pieces were quite large and angular and were snugged tightly together, so it took me considerable time and effort to break my way through and discover, concealed behind them, a new hole. This was a handsome, almost circular opening, right through the baseboard into the main room of the store. Cunning, or perhaps just lucky, the industrious ancestors had driven it through just behind an old iron safe, at a spot practically invisible to any people in the shop. The Balcony and the Balloon, precious as they were, amounted only to lookouts, observatories suspended like aeries above the mingle and fray of the business, and had not given me actual entrance to the store and to its vast trove of fresh books, as did this new discovery. With what I thought was a fine sense of deliberate irony, I named it the Rathole. I could have named it the Gate of Heaven.

After that I pretty much abandoned the basement for the superior books upstairs. Room after room of them. Some were bound in leather, their pages edged with gold, though I personally preferred paperbacks, especially the ones from New Directions, with their black-and-white covers, and the serious, austere ones from Scribner's. If I were a person reading in a park I would always carry one of those. The basement had been good to me, but it was upstairs that I really felt myself blossoming. My intellect grew sharper than my teeth. Soon I could do a four-hundred-page novel in an hour, knock off Spinoza in a day. Sometimes I would gaze around me and tremble with joy. I could not understand why this had been granted me. Sometimes I imagined it was part of a secret plan. I thought, Could it be that I, despite my unlikely appearance, have a Destiny? And by that I meant the sort of thing people have in stories, where the events of a life, no matter how they churn and swirl, are swirled and churned in the end into a kind of pattern. Lives in stories have direction and meaning. Even stupid, meaningless lives, like Lenny's in *Of Mice and Men*, acquire through their place in a story at least the dignity and meaning of being Stupid, Meaningless Lives, the consolation of being exemplars of something. In real life you do not get even that.

I have never been very brave in a physical way, or in any other way either, and I have had a hard time facing up to the blank stupidity of an ordinary, unstoried life, so I very early on started comforting myself with the ridiculous idea that I really did have a Destiny. And I began to travel, in space and time, in my books, looking for it. I dropped in on Daniel Defoe in London for a guided tour of the plague. I heard the bell ringer calling, 'Bring out your dead,' and I smelled the smoke from the burning corpses. It is in my nostrils still. People were dying like rats all over London – in fact the rats were dying too, like people. After a couple of hours of this I needed a change of scene, so I went to China and climbed a steep narrow path through bamboo and cypress, to sit for a while in the open doorway of a small mountain but with old Tu Fu. Staring silently out at the white mist swirling up from the valley, listening to the wind blowing through the reed curtains and the faint reverberations of distant temple bells, we were each 'alone with ten thousand things.' After that I shot back to England – hopping over oceans, continents, and centuries as easily as stepping off a curb – where I built a small fire by a cart road so that poor, doomed Tess, grubbing turnips in a bleak windswept field, could warm her chapped hands. I had read her life twice through to the end already – I knew her Destiny – and I turned my face away to hide the tears. Then I journeyed with Marlow aboard a ragged steamer up a river in Africa looking for a man named Kurtz. We found him all right. Better for us that we hadn't! And I introduced people. I put Baudelaire on the raft with Huck and Jim. It did him a lot of good. And sometimes I made sad people happier. I let Keats marry Fanny before he died. I couldn't save him, but you should have seen them on their wedding night, in a cheap *pensione* in Rome. To them it was a fairy palace. I let the books enter my dreams, and sometimes I dreamed myself back into the books. I held Natasha Rostova's tiny waist, felt her hand resting on my shoulder, and we danced, seeming to float on the swells of the waltz, right across the gleaming parquet of the ballroom and out into a garden hung with paper lanterns, while the dashing lieutenants of the Imperial Guard furiously twisted their mustaches.

You laugh. You are right to laugh. I was once – despite my unpleasant mien – a hopeless romantic, that most ridiculous of creatures. And a humanist too, equally hopeless. And yet despite – or is it because? – of these failings I was able to meet a lot of fabulous people and a lot of geniuses too in the course of my early education. I got on conversational terms with all the Big Ones. Dostoyevsky and Strindberg, for example. In them I was quick to recognize fellow sufferers, hysterics like me. And from them I learned a valuable lesson – that no matter how small you are, your madness can be as big as anyone's.

And you don't have to believe stories to love them. I love all stories. I love the progression of beginning, middle, and end. I love the slow accumulation of meaning, the misty landscapes of the imagination, the mazy walks, the wooded slopes, the reflecting pools, the tragic twists and comic stumbles. The only literature I cannot abide is rat literature, including mouse literature. I despise good-natured old Ratty in *The Wind in the Willows*. I piss down the throats of Mickey Mouse and Stuart Little. Affable, shuffling, *cute*, they stick in my craw like fish bones.

And now, at the end of it all, I cannot make myself believe anymore that many real people have Destinies, and I am sure that rats never do.

Despite my intelligence, my tact, the delicacy and refinement of my feelings, my growing erudition, I remained a creature of great disabilities. Reading is one thing, speaking is another, and I don't mean public speaking. I do not mean that I suffered from social phobia, though that was in fact the case. No, I mean actual vocal utterance – of that I was not capable. Loquacious to the point of chatter, I was condemned to silence. The fact is, I had no voice. All the beautiful sentences flying around in my head like butterflies were in fact flying in a cage they could never get out of. All the lovely words that I mulled and mouthed in the strangled silence of my thought were as useless as the thousands, perhaps millions, of words that I had torn from books and swallowed, the incohesive fragments of entire novels, plays, epic poems, intimate diaries, and scandalous confessions – all down the tube, mute, useless, and wasted. The problem is physiological: I don't have the right kind of vocal cords. I spent hours declaiming Shakespeare's lines. I was never able to get beyond a few incomprehensible variations on the basic squeak. Here is Hamlet, dagger in hand: *squeak squeak squeak*. (And there is Firmin crushed beneath a barrage of boos and seat cushions.) I do better with the lines where Macbeth talks of life being a tale told by an idiot, signifying nothing: a few pathetic squeaks serve pretty well there. Oh, what a clown! I laugh, in order not to weep – which, of course, I also cannot do. Or laugh either, for that matter, except in my head, where it is more painful than tears.

It was during the period of tunnel exploration – I was still very young, having scarcely graduated from the children's classics and possessing only a shaky grasp of the world – that I saw myself in a mirror for the first time. The door under RESTROOM carried a handwritten sign that said PLEASE

KEEP THIS DOOR CLOSED. And people did. After the noise of rushing water and before the sound of footsteps on the stairs, there had always intervened the forbidding click of a latch. I was in the corner behind the water heater the day the silence fell, louder than any click, between the flushing and the footfalls. I knew right away what had happened, and when the shop closed that evening I crept out into the flickering. The door under RESTROOM stood open, and a light was on in the small chamber beyond, brighter than anything I had ever imagined. At first I was dazzled by the light and bewildered by the porcelain figures within. These closely resembled the altars I had seen in *A Child's Picture Bible*, and I assumed I was entering some sort of temple. The smooth white surfaces and the shiny silver fixtures seemed very solemn. (At that age I still had difficulty distinguishing between solemn and sanitary.) I first explored the rim of an oval basin half-filled with water, its interior streaked with brown stains, and then I nibbled a bit from a roll of soft white paper attached to the wall beside it – it tasted like Emily Post. From there I was able to jump to the high altar, which turned out to be another basin, but empty this time, with a round silver-rimmed hole at the bottom. Above it, slanting slightly downward, hung a large metal-framed mirror in which the room behind me tilted crazily. Though my intellect was still fairly undeveloped, I grasped immediately the principle of the thing. I stood on my hind legs on the basin's outer rim, and by stretching my body up as high as I could I managed to see myself plain for the first time. I had of course seen the members of my family, and I suppose I really ought to have been able to infer my own appearance from theirs. Yet we differed in so many important ways, I had assumed – willfully assumed, I now realized – that we would differ in this respect also.

In the end, seeing myself for the first time was not at all like seeing just any old rat. The experience was more personal, and more painful too. While it was easy enough to gaze at the unlovely shapes of Shunt or Peewee, it was horrible to have to look upon my own similar aspect. I realized, of course, that the intensity of this pain was in exact proportion to the enormity of my vanity, but that thought only made things worse. Not just ugly, but vain as well – which only added ridiculous to the pile. There I stood, tilted slightly, in irrefutable detail – short, thick-waisted, hairy, and chinless. Firmin: fur-man. Ridiculous. The chin, or the lack thereof, caused me special pain. It seemed to point – though in fact this nonentity was incapable of anything as bold as pointing – to a gross lack of moral fiber. And I thought the dark bulging eyes gave me a revoltingly froglike air. It was, in short, a shifty, dishonest face, untrustworthy, the face of a really low character. Firmin the vermin. But the details – no chin, pointy nose, yellow teeth, etc. – were not important in themselves when compared to the overall impression of ugliness. Even back then, when my ideas of beauty reached no further than Tenniel's drawings of Alice, I knew that *this* was ugly. And the contrast, the heartbreakingly unbridgeable *distance*, became only greater when later on I became aware of truly beautiful

creatures like Ginger, Fred, Rita, Gary, Ava, and all the Lovelies. It was not tolerable.

From then on I went to great lengths to avoid my own reflection. It was easy to stay away from mirrors, but windows and hubcaps were a different story. Whenever I caught a glimpse of myself in one of those, I was instantly horrified, as if I had seen a monster. Of course I quickly recognized that the monster was just myself again, and I cannot describe the grief I then felt. So I developed a little mental trick: whenever this happened, instead of saying 'that's me' and bursting into tears, I would say 'that's him' and run away.

During those early days, and especially after I had won access to the main floor, I burned the candle at both ends, and except for the times when hunger drove me out into the world to scrounge for food, I used up most of my night hours reading and traveling in the bookshop and spent the better part of every day glued to the Balloon or the Balcony, fearful of missing something of the goings-on below. Twice I was so tired at night that I fell asleep on a book, and each time woke with a start at the rattle of a key in the front door – Norman was opening the shop – only to dive through the Rathole in the nick of time. And once, nodding off at my post, I almost fell out of the Balloon.

It was from the Balloon that, some weeks earlier, I had glimpsed Norman for the first time. I had not glimpsed all of Norman though, just the shiny dome of his head, and the tops of his shoulders and arms. He was not Norman yet either, he was still just the Owner of the Desk. It had taken me a long time to screw up the courage to peer down from the Balloon during store hours. But then early one morning I finally managed. Hearing no sound from below but the plaintive creaking of the chair and an occasional rattle of paper, I placed a cautious eye at the rim of the Confidential Crack, and I saw him there at the desk. Elbows on the chair arms, he was reading a newspaper. With my amazing eyesight I could read the paper as well, but at that moment I was more interested in reading what was written on Norman's bald head. My life has been marked by a series of extraordinary coincidences – for a long time I took these as further signs that I was in possession of a Destiny – and it so happened that just before I looked down on Norman's head for the first time I had been learning a thing or two about skull-reading.

I had been working under RARE BOOKS AND FIRST EDITIONS for the previous week or so and had spent part of the previous night hunched over Franz Joseph Gall's *The Anatomy and Physiology of the Nervous System in General, and of the Brain in Particular*, a groundbreaking work on phrenology. While I was skeptical at first that a person's character could be read from the bumps and dimples on his skull, a systematic palpation of my own furry pate – by means of a forepaw – had disclosed large protuberances (amounting almost to deformations) right where you would expect them. The bulge on my forehead – a wartlike knob I habitually rub when puzzled – is indicative, according to Gall, of prodigious linguistic endowment, while the sad-sack ridges below my eye sockets are signs of an

elevated 'spiritual' temperament. I also discovered at the base of my skull telltale bulges for 'adhesiveness' and 'amativeness,' indicating the presence – and can I deny it? – of 'a tendency to form strong attachments to others' and 'a proclivity to lust and carnal appetite.' Finally, just to show that even a skull is capable of a little irony, I bear on my temples small but unmistakable ridges produced by the outward thrust of irrepressible Hope.

Peering over the edge of the Balloon, I mapped the hills and dales of Norman's bean. Posted there as plain as day were the signs of intelligence, spirituality, mental energy, firmness, and – this was the best of all – a regular hillock pointing to 'philoprogenitiveness,' defined by Gall as a 'particular feeling that leads one to watch over and provide for helpless offspring.' This discovery of the true nature of the Owner of the Desk filled me with happiness – for the first time in my life I did not feel alone in the world. It gave me a sense of security and – as Gall might have put it – a strong feeling of adhesiveness. I was instantly in love.

Here I seem to hear sounds of impatience, a pointed shifting of a chair, a deliberate snort. The sight of my happiness, I suppose, goads you into pointing out the painfully obvious, and you wonder aloud if it had never occurred to me that I might not exactly belong to the category of 'helpless offspring.' The short answer to that one is: never. Looking back I can see that the whole near-tragedy, which I shall get to shortly, was caused by the simple fact that Norman's head was not entirely hairless. My investigation of his character, however diligent, was blunted by an ill-kempt growth of dark curls shrouding his temples. Had I been able to perch on a shoulder and explore those temples with my forepaws I have no doubt as to what I would have found: crescent-shaped ridges over the ears, indicating 'destructiveness,' aided and abetted by a pair of wedge-shaped bulges, pointing to 'secretiveness.' But all that was in the future. For now it is appropriate to place beneath the picture of Norman at his desk the caption THE FIRST HUMAN BEING F. EVER LOVED.

Chapter 5

I traveled in my books but I no longer ate them, and food – the mundane, illiterate kind – was a constant problem. I was forced to leave the shop every night, ramp up my courage and creep out under the cellar door, to forage around the Square, cringing in shadows, creeping down drains, racing from dark spot to dark spot. *Diary of a Nightcrawler.* As the year wore on, the days growing colder, then warmer, I began to notice changes in the neighborhood, and I don't mean the stunted flowerings of a few ragged clumps of grass and daffodils. Indeed, the changes I am referring to stood in ironic contrast to those meager burgeonings. On nearly every block businesses were vanishing, and at night the side streets, and even the Square itself, emptied out earlier. Apart from the knots of sailors in the doorways of bars, there was often no one around after eleven. There were more broken windows in the buildings, and these often went unmended or were replaced by plywood sheets. Trash piled up in alleys and even on the sidewalks in front of some stores. Cars were abandoned at the curb, to be slowly picked to pieces by scavengers, and the brick buildings themselves seemed to sag with age, as though, like old people or old rats, they had lost the will to hold themselves erect. Rats moved into the cars, building cozy burrows in the seats.

Now and then I bumped into one of the old bunch out there. They too had changed a lot since setting out on their own. Hollow-cheeked and furtive, long bodies and hanging bellies, they were unpleasant-looking characters – to the point where I almost didn't recognize them. They usually liked pretending they didn't know me either. They were always frantic to get someplace or other – chasing rumors of easy grub or running from the Man – but occasionally one of them would stop to bat the breeze, give me the news and maybe a tip about where I could scarf up some supper. The tips were usually false, designed to send me off in the wrong direction. Deep down they had not changed much – in their eyes I was still a prize chump. It was through one of those chance encounters that I found out Peewee had been killed, run over by a taxi the night before. I stood with Shunt on the sidewalk while he pointed out a patch of fur in the middle of Cambridge Street, like a little rug. Though Peewee had never shown me the slightest consideration, it was unnerving to see him like that. In my mind, I posted next to his name the words RIDICULOUS and LIFE.

And what did I post next to my own name? When I was in the dumps, I posted GROTESQUE CLOWN and even RAT, but when I was up – which was often the case back then – I posted BUSINESSMAN. My business was books – consumption and exchange. I hung out in the Balloon and the Balcony and studied the trade. I leaned over the edge of the Balloon, in constant peril of falling, and read the morning paper over Norman's shoulder. At times, when he placed his coffee cup just so, I could see my own reflection in the dark water – not an appetizing sight at breakfast time. Norman was a real reader too. He would feel about on the desk for his cup like a blind man, find it, grasp it, and raise it to his lips without ever taking his eyes off the newspaper. The aroma of coffee floated up and hung around the ceiling. I loved that smell, though it would be a long time before I actually tasted coffee.

A man in a bar once asked me what books taste like 'in an average sort of way.' I had a ready answer, but in order not to make him feel completely stupid, I pretended to ponder the question for a while before saying, 'My friend, given the chasm that separates all your experiences from all of mine, I can bring you no closer to that singular savor than by saying that books, in an average sort of way, taste the way coffee smells.' This was a mouthful, and I could tell by the way he returned to his drink that I had given him plenty to think about. Now that I am alone again, I don't ever smell coffee anymore, which is one more nice thing gone from my life.

After the morning paper, I would eavesdrop on Norman's dealings with his customers. Many – perhaps most – were true readers hoping to buy a few good books cheap. If they had not come in with a title on their lips or if their browsing seemed unfocused and vague, Norman was sure to notice, and he always knew how to steer them in the right direction. He was a real Sherlock Holmes when it came to the divination of character from outward appearances. He could tell at a glance – from their dress, their accents, their haircuts, even their gaits – the kind of books they liked, and he never made a mistake, never handed *Peyton Place* to someone who would have been happier with *Doctor Zhivago*. Nor vice versa – Norman Shine was not a snob. He was short and big-bottomed. He had a broad face – it seemed to be wider than it was long – and a very small mouth, which he would purse up when he listened. Ask him a question, ask him if he has *Dombey and Son* or Marivaux's *Life of Marianne* in translation, and watch his mouth draw up. It was like pulling the string of a little sack or poking a sea anemone. And no matter how ordinary the question – 'Who wrote *War and Peace?*' or 'Where is your restroom?' – he would incline his head so as to look at you over the tops of his glasses, purse his lips, and in general act as if yours was the most profound of inquiries. Then the anemone would forget its fear, the drawstring would relax, his mouth would open in the gentlest of smiles, and raising an extended index finger as if testing the wind, he would say, 'Back room, left-hand shelves, third shelf from the bottom, toward the end,' or some such precise thing. With his bald pate and horseshoe of bushy hair, he looked like a jolly friar. I sometimes mixed him up with Friar Tuck.

On Saturday afternoons, especially when the weather was fine, the shop would be crowded with customers, and Norman would leave his desk by the door and move about the store helping people find what they wanted. He was beautiful then, moving gracefully among them. He was like a musketeer. He was Athos, quiet and reserved, slow to anger, but deadly when provoked. Assaulted by a question from behind, he spins about, thrusts his rapier at a top shelf, and draws down, impaled and flashing like a fish on a spear, *Death in Venice*. Another request might send him charging down an aisle, a turn at the corner of a shelf, a left feint in the direction of juvenilia, and then, crouching, a lunge to the right – and there, skewered by his sword point, is *Betty Crocker's Picture Cook Book*. A third request, this time from an old woman in a mackintosh, bent and ugly, meets with the usual deference. A deep bow, a chivalrous pirouette, two lightning jabs, and *The Power of Positive Thinking* and *Arthritis and Common Sense* lie at her feet. Bravo, mon vieux Athos, bravo.

But Norman's most endearing moments occurred on rainy days, with no customers in the store, when he roamed the aisles armed with a large turkey-feather duster, and dusted to the right, dusted to the left, and hummed or whistled as he went. Seeing him then made me think how nice it was to be human. Rainy days were pleasant ones for me too. Lulled by the watery pit-a-pat, I occasionally dozed off at my post. And sometimes I had nightmares in which I died excruciating deaths, crushed beneath *Webster's* unabridged or flushed screaming down a drain. And then I would wake up in the warm store to the gentle hissing of the rain and the whispering of the feather duster and feel happy again.

Meanwhile, the world outside the bookstore was looking more and more like a place I did not much

want to be part of. During our orientation trip up top Mama had complained a lot to Luweena and me about our lack of gratitude for all she was doing for us in showing us the great scrape-and-scrounge spots. Which was ridiculous. From my point of view she had shown us mostly a bunch of death traps and not much to be grateful for. The one exception was the Rialto Theater, and for that even to this day my gratitude knows no bounds. No Rialto, no longing. No longing, no Lovelies. No Lovelies, and . . . what? No Lovelies, and a lonely rodent, at the closing of the garden, mulling the quality of his despair. The rest of my family were blessed in a way. Thanks to their dwarfish imaginations and short memories they did not ask for a lot, mostly just food and fornication, and they got enough of both to take them through life while it lasted. But that was not the life for me. Like an idiot, I had aspirations. And besides, I was terrified. The Rialto stood out as the one moderately safe place in the whole depressing neighborhood where you could still pick up something to eat, and eat it calmly without worrying about what calamity was going to fall on your head and turn you into a rug like Peewee. A combination movie theater and flophouse, the Rialto stayed open twenty-four hours a day. Half the audience was there only to sleep – it was cheaper than a room and warmer than a street. It was known affectionately as the Scratch House, and most rats avoided it because of the vermin, a voracious population of fleas and lice, and also because of the reek – a stench of old people, poor people, sweat and jism, mixed with the stink of the pesticides and disinfectants they dumped in once a week. But to me, given my temperament, that seemed a small price to pay. The Rialto screened old movies during the day and evening, perhaps forty films in all, which it continuously recirculated, in order to maintain a front of shabby respectability. Then at midnight, when the citizenry and its censors were tucked in bed and the cops could safely look the other way, it would switch over to pornography. At the stroke of midnight, a halt, scratched, and flickering Charlie Chan or Gene Autry would come to a clattering stop in midreel. Utter darkness would follow, a few short minutes of coughing and shuffling, and then the projector would whirr back to life, and even its sound would seem younger, brighter. The change was spectacular.

Though the Rialto had a lot to offer, attendance was always sparse, and I found it easy to creep down the empty rows and with finikin discernment harvest the choicest bits of candy bar and popcorn and even an occasional serving of hot dog or smoked ham (the all-nighters often brought lunch with them) while the projector's beam flashed like a searchlight above me. This profusion of provender, however, was for me not foremost among the Rialto's attractions. For there on the midnight screen, naked and enormous as Amazons, were creatures just like the ones who had transfixed me with their loveliness in front of the Casino weeks before. But here they did not wear black rectangles on their chests and thighs, nor were they frozen in photographic stillness. Here they moved like real creatures in living color and danced and sometimes writhed on carpets that had obviously been made from animals far furrier than Peewee. They writhed alone or with men – whose gross presence, muscled and sinewed like enormous baby rats, I personally found superfluous and offensive – and sometimes they writhed in each other's arms. How I longed for that smooth skin like soft chamois – to smell it, touch it, taste it; and that thick flowing hair – to bury my face in it, to swoon. I was well aware of what the others of my putative species, the few who might venture in, would think of these velvet-skinned beings. Where I discerned angels, they would see only hideous upright animals, lumbering, hairless, and vain. And if they did not laugh, it would be only because they never do.

The pull of these tremendous and fascinating creatures was so strong that I found myself sacrificing hours and even days at the bookstore just to behold them. I haul out my telescope once again. Trembling with impatience, I wait for my eyes to grow accustomed to the flickering darkness. Peering into that Rialto of dream and memory, I sweep my telescope this way and that until I find the younger me, the careless progenitor of this present wreck, locked in the circle of the lens: I am holding a little piece of what looks like a Snickers and I am perched on a seat in the front row among the drunken snorers, the mendicant munchers, the droolers, and the masturbators. Chewing quietly I contemplate the slow disrobings, the tentative undulations, the wild gyrations of the beings I have come to think of simply as 'my Lovelies.' Chew and

contemplate, contemplate and chew, utterly rapt, utterly happy. I am not ashamed. Sometimes I think that all anyone needs in life is lots of popcorn and a few Lovelies.

Norman acquired most of his books at estate sales, and that for me was the only sad part of the book business. Returning from one of these sales, the old wood-paneled Buick wagon would be so weighed down with books that when he backed up to the shop door the bumper would scrape on the sidewalk. Opening the rear gate, he would carry them inside by the armful and stack them next to his desk in waist-high piles and during the days that followed open them one by one and pencil a price on the inside. I hated that part of the business. I hated most of all reading the inscriptions over his shoulder: 'For my darling Peter on our fiftieth wedding anniversary' (in *The Rubáiyát of Omar Khayyám*), 'This book was given me by dear dead Violet Swain when we were both seventeen' (in *The Catcher in the Rye*), 'To Mary, may it bring her solace' (in John Donne's *Sermons*), 'Just to remind you of our fortnight of Italian heaven' (in Ruskin's *The Stones of Venice*), 'Madness is only misunderstood genius – pray for me' (in Blake's *Songs of Innocence and of Experience*), 'I live, I die; I have lived, I am dead; I shall die, I will live' (in Kierkegaard's *Fear and Trembling*). Dozens of these in every carload. It was obscene. They should have buried the books with their owners, like the Egyptians, just so people couldn't paw over them afterward

– give them something to read on the long ride through eternity.

Most books got priced at less than a dollar, though Norman had an eye for real value too, and – what with the bumps above his ears – a gift for secrecy. When he spotted a truly valuable book at one of those estate sales, he kept it up his sleeve until he had bought it for a song. He might pay a nickel for a book and then turn around, stick it in a glass-fronted case, and sell it for a thousand dollars the next day. When the collectors came in to see what he had, they put on white cotton gloves before touching anything in the case. And some of these were books that Norman had been schlepping around in his station wagon a few days before. But don't tell that to the collectors! They sat there as solemn as Popes with their white gloves on, holding a book as gently as if it were a newborn baby, and talked about provenance, first printings, autographs, and the great Rosenbach. Some of these people knew a lot about the history of books, but none of them knew as much as Norman, and they could never put anything over on him. He was amazing. I came to believe that he knew everything. In my mind I had long since taken down the sign that labeled him as merely the Owner of the Desk, and next to his name I had put up two new signs: THE SWORDSMAN and THE BEARER OF THE KEY OF KNOWLEDGE. It was an easy step, via the image of the key, from there to St. Peter. And that was how the image of Norman Shine got mixed up in my mind with the idea of sainthood.

There was another interesting aspect of the book

business, one that brought Norman closer to the hidden projectionist at the Rialto. You see, besides the good used books on the shelves and the very used books in the basement and the rare books in the glass-fronted cabinets, there were also books in the old iron safe in front of the Rathole. These were the banned books, white-covered paperbacks published by Olympia Press and Obelisk Press and smuggled in from Paris. They had titles like *Tropic of Cancer, Our Lady of the Flowers, The Ginger Man, Naked Lunch, My Life and Loves*. The customers for these books spoke the names in whispers. If Norman knew the customer, or after sizing him up (they were all men) decided to trust him, off would come the Friar Tuck disguise: Norman's round eyes would narrow, his little pocketbook mouth would flatten to a hard slit. It was like watching a different movie – here was the secret agent of the French underground handing out forged papers, or perhaps an underworld fence passing stolen diamonds. 'Just a moment,' he would say, and he would shoot a quick glance around. Then, crouching in front of the safe so as to hide its contents from view, he would deftly angle the contraband into a plain brown bag, one without PEMBROKE BOOKS written on it, but not before a whiff of Paris – Gauloise Bleu and red wine and car exhaust – had wafted up from the open safe to mingle with the coffee smell on the ceiling. And I thought, Good old Norman, striking a blow for freedom. Which shows that even before meeting Jerry Magoon I was a revolutionary at heart. It also shows that I was hiding from myself the obvious fact that,

besides the blow for freedom, Norman was making a killing. He was, I now understand, a mixed character. But in those days the only mixed character I had an eye for was myself.

All these new experiences got a tremendous battle going in my mind between Pembroke Books and the Rialto. To me they were like rival temples vying for my worship – sages and arhats on the one hand, angels on the other. Sometimes I gave in to the one and sometimes I gave in to the other. And when I gave in to the Rialto side I would often stay on right through the night. That way I could catch the daytime features without having to walk the streets in daylight. Among the continuously recycled black-and-white movies, besides Charlie Chan and Gene Autry, were westerns, gangster movies, and musicals, films with Joan Fontaine, Paulette Godard, James Cagney, Abbott and Costello, and Fred Astaire. The projectionist must have had a soft spot for Fred Astaire, he showed so many of his movies, and it was not long before I had a soft spot for him too. When his movies were showing I always stayed on. I was sure the projectionist was another guardian of the mysteries, like Norman. Two temples, two priests. I longed to catch a glimpse of him, but I never did.

Fred Astaire became my shining example – his walk, his talk, his tastes. So I naturally developed a soft spot for Ginger Rogers too, and I put her in with my Lovelies. It happened now and then that a movie with her in it was the last thing showing before the apotheosis at midnight. Dressed in a floating gown and clasping

Astaire's outstretched hand, the bejeweled and apparently weightless Ginger, suspended in *arabesque penché*, would suddenly vanish, wrapped in a cloud of night like Eurydice. And I, huddled in the coughing, shuffling darkness that had swallowed her up, would imagine that she had disappeared forever. And I experienced real – not imagined – grief. In fact, I would manage to work up a pretty good head of emotional steam, when suddenly, accompanied by the whirr of the projector – a sound that had become as stirring as Wagner's *Ride of the Valkyries* – there she would be again, back from the dead, naked and assumed into heaven, writhing on a rug. It was magical. I longed to approach her as a supplicant, a stemless rose in my paws, and humbly place the blossom in the little vase of her navel, like an offering. But I guess all that emotion, all that yearning, was too enormous for my little frame to bear, and on those nights, coming home to my dusty hovel in the ceiling of the bookshop, I would grow terribly depressed. Unrequited love is bad, but unrequitable love can really get you down.

I wouldn't eat for two days. I would read Byron. I would read *Wuthering Heights*. I changed my name to Heathcliff. I lay on my back. I looked at my toes. After that I would throw myself into my work with increased energy. I was Jay Gatsby. I showed a great capacity for bouncing back. I carried on with business. Outwardly I was my old affable self, and who could know that I was hiding a broken heart?

Every morning Norman and I read the *Boston Globe*. We read it all the way through, including the want ads. I became informed about the world, I became a well-informed citizen, and when the paper referred to 'the general public,' I felt a little pang of narcissistic pride. I learned to orient myself in space: when I stood facing the glass cabinet my nose drove a wedge toward Provincetown across the bay, and my tail sent a spear along Route 2 to Fitchburg. And in time: just behind me lay the election of a Catholic as president of the United States, the crash of a spy plane in Russia, a massacre in South Africa, while in front of me, according to the *Globe*, loomed nuclear annihilation, shorter skirts, and a lot of new movies.

Closer to home, I learned how the Red Sox were doing and about the plans for the disappearance of Scollay Square. Disappearance by means of the persistent application of heavy machinery. This was a hard thing to read about, especially for me. After all, this was the only life I had ever known. Where would I be without the bookstore, without the Rialto? And I could tell it was hard on Norman too, because he talked about it a lot. He talked about it with tall, balding Alvin Sweat, owner of Sweat's Sweets next door, and with adipose and balding George Vahradyan, who ran an amalgamation of drugstore and carpet emporium across the street called Drugs and Rugs. Some days, according to the *Globe*, the destruction was imminent, and some days it was projected, and some days it was impending. On rainy days, when there were no customers, it must have been just plain threatening, because on those days the three bald heads would bob around Norman's desk below the Balloon, drink his coffee, talk about what was going to happen – and when it was going to happen and what in God's name they were going to do after it had happened – and complain. Alvin had a weakness for colorful language and George had a weakness for big cigars, and standing around the desk talking to Norman, Alvin's 'flying fucks,' 'asses from elbows,' and 'busted nuts,' would mingle with George's cigar smoke and both would float up to the ceiling, where they mixed with the smells of coffee and Paris. These conversations naturally did nothing to save the neighborhood, and they usually left Norman and me so depressed we would just bury ourselves in work, taking out books and wiping them with a cloth, if nothing else. That was, of course, Norman. As for me, I lay on my back in bed and worked on my poem 'Ode to Night.' It began 'Hail, Darkness.'

The neighborhood – which the *Globe* sometimes called 'historic' but more often referred to as 'blighted' and even 'rat infested' (true!) – was a bulwark in the path of progress, so the mayor and the city council wanted to move it out of the way, and it seemed that the best way of doing that would be to flatten it and then cover it over with cement. The *Globe* published some drawings of how Boston was going to look when they finished, when it would gleam like Miami across the gray waters of the harbor. They planned to replace Scollay Square with a large flat piece of concrete, and on top of that, to frighten people, they were going to put government buildings, like forts. Norman looked at the pictures of the buildings in the paper and just shook his head. And above him in the Balloon I shook my head too.

Destroying that much of the city was going to be a big job. The buildings were old and had deep roots and did not want to go. So the mayor and the city council went looking for the right man, someone who understood the difficulties of applying heavy machinery to very old buildings and narrow streets, and they found Edward Logue. He was nicknamed the Bombardier, because that was what he had been during World War II. In a B-24. So he had had firsthand experience with the largest urban renewal project in human history. He sent the mayor and the city council pictures of Stuttgart and Dresden and told them, 'I can make Scollay Square look like that.' He got the job. They put a huge photo of him in the paper, standing next to the mayor. They were holding hands, but they were not looking at each other – they were smiling at the camera. Logue was the man for the cataclysm. When I saw the picture, I couldn't stop myself from dressing him up in the uniform of the Wehrmacht, and then I promoted him to general. And so life wore on. We kept one eye on the business and one on General Logue, and a sense of doom began to gather around us like a poison mist.

Chapter 6

Pembroke Books was a very well-known bookshop, the kind of place famous people sometimes visit. More than once I had heard Norman tell about how Jack Kennedy, who had become president of the United States, used to drop in for coffee and a chat when he was just a congressman, and also Ted Williams, who was a famous hitter for the Red Sox. I didn't care much about them. But Norman also liked to tell people about the time the famous playwright Arthur Miller stopped in to buy a copy of his own play. I wished I could have been there. I kept hoping he would come back, or if not him somebody else – John Steinbeck, Robert Frost, or even Grace Metalious. None of them lived that far away. And then there was Robert Lowell, who lived around the corner. But he never came either.

Only one writer ever came in during my tenure and he was a disappointment at first. He was not famous yet, and Alvin, talking to Norman one day when the writer had just left the shop, called him 'that bohemian character.' At that time I was still in my bourgeois phase and so this was not yet an appellation that I aspired to. Norman also once described him as an experimental novelist, though he might have meant

that as a joke. At other times he called him a crackpot and a drunk. This writer lived upstairs from the bookstore, though I did not know that yet – I did not even know there was an upstairs. You reached his place through a doorway between Pembroke Books and the Tattoo Palace. This doorway was under ROOMS and the door itself had frosted glass on its top half and DR LIEBERMAN PAINLESS DENTIST written in a semicircle of gold letters on the glass. Usually when this writer stopped in the store he was on his way someplace else, often faraway places like Harvard Square across the river in Cambridge, and he was going there on a very old bicycle with a large wire basket in front. It had green fenders and between the bars a little white button for the horn. I don't know if the horn worked. He often left the bicycle leaning against the store window, despite the fact that Norman had asked him not to. I did not know how to admire that trait yet, so I took Norman's side and at first did not feel a lot of respect for this writer. He was not at all a young man and I thought he had better hurry if he was going to be famous. That's how bourgeois I was. He was the only man I had ever seen with hair to his shoulders. It was gray and thinning and bound at the top by a blue headband like an Indian's. Otherwise he did not look anything like an Indian. His name was Jerry Magoon. He was a short stocky man with a big head. He had a small Irish nose, a big drooping mustache over a wide thin-lipped mouth, and blue eyes, one of which was always staring off to the side. People could never be sure if he was looking at them or not. And he always wore the same rumpled blue suit and black knit tie. This gave him an oddly contradictory appearance, as if on the one hand he was trying to be neat and proper and on the other hand he was sleeping in his clothes.

Except for the suit and tie, he looked like a prospector in one of the Rialto westerns and before I learned his name I always called him the Prospector. Later I called him the Smartest Man in the World. He came often during my tenure at the store. He was one of the regulars, and he always hung around a long time, usually in the basement, where the cheapest books were, pulling volumes out of the shelves, leafing through them, and putting them back, and sometimes, when he found one he liked, he would read it all the way through just standing there. While he read he mumbled to himself and wagged his big head. It was a long bike ride to Cambridge and he was a pretty old man, so I supposed he was in no hurry to get going. And Norman didn't seem to mind. After a while it occurred to me that Norman was in fact quite fond of the writer, so I got fond of him too.

He sometimes helped Norman unload the station wagon full of books, and once Norman paid him to wash the front windows. He did a good job. Usually he did not buy anything – he was obviously very poor – but one day in early spring he left with a big bag full of books. I could not see what was in the bag, but that evening I was able to reconstruct it from the gaps in the shelves. It was all religion and science fiction: Buber's *The Way of Man: According to the Teaching of Hasidism*, Asimov's *The Stars, like Dust*, Van Vogt's *The Weapon Shops of Isher*, Bultmann's *History and Eschatology*, and Heinlein's *Citizen of the Galaxy*. These were some of my own favorite works. On a later visit he went off with every book we had on insects. And Norman asked him that time, while he was packing them up, what he was working on those days. I nearly fell out of the Balloon when I heard his answer.

'I got a new novel going,' he said, 'about a rat. The furry kind. They're really going to hate this one.'

Norman laughed. 'A sequel?' he asked.

And Jerry answered, 'No, this is something entirely different. I'm through with that kind of obvious stuff. You got to keep moving, you know. Like sharks. You stop and you drown.'

Apparently Norman did know, because he just nodded and handed Jerry his books.

From then on, whenever a new batch of books arrived I tore through it looking for Jerry Magoon's novel. Miracles do happen – I was sure of that. In fact I acknowledged it every time I arrived safely home from the Square, when I let a sigh of gratitude for one more miracle granted float up in the general direction of heaven, and I acknowledged it again the night I laid paws on the novel. It was a cheaply printed paperback of 227 yellowing pages. On the cover, against a canary yellow background, New York City was in flames, while wreathed in smoke above the blazing skyline loomed an enormous rat, bigger than the Empire State Building, with red eyes and dripping red fangs. The title appeared in blood red strokes at the top of the page: *The Nesting*. And at the bottom, in letters that struck me as insultingly small, was the name E. J. Magoon. I realized after reading the book that the folks at Astral Press, which had published it in 1950, had possessed a real gift for hyperbole – the book in fact did not contain any giant rats, though it did have plenty of burning cities toward the end.

For a century prior to the present age, the gentle and enormously intelligent inhabitants of Axi 12, a planet located at the far edge of our galaxy, had been sending robotic probes to study the planet Earth, which was the only planet in the whole galaxy apart from their own inhabited by advanced life-forms. These probes had collected an enormous amount of data on Earth and its creatures, and the Axions believed that the time had come to initiate actual contact with earthlings, though they knew this would not be easy. Axions, while far more advanced than earthlings, both ethically and intellectually, had the misfortune from an earthling's point of view of looking like garden slugs. They were also the size of Shetland ponies. Being quite intelligent, they had the good sense to recognize that their appearance might give earthlings wrong ideas about the Axions' superior morals and intellects. It was even conceivable that the earthlings might refuse to make friends with pony-sized slugs. Luckily, these superior sluglike creatures were also in possession of advanced protoplasmic morphing techniques, and they decided to send to Earth an exploratory expedition made up of a dozen Axions who had been previously morphed into the shape of Earth's dominant species. Furthermore, in order that these explorers might learn to fully understand the earthlings' customs and language prior to initiating contact, they were sent as infants, extraterrestrial changelings, to be reared by unwitting Earth mothers as their own. Hence the book's title. When these changelings reached adulthood, masters of Earth's language and customs, with friends and associates – and even siblings and parents – among the dominant species, they would be perfectly placed to serve as mediators between earthlings and Axions.

It seemed like a good plan, but unfortunately, despite the decades of orbital snooping and analysis, the Axions' robotic probes had made a stupid mistake, wrongly concluding that the earth's dominant species was the Norway rat. As a consequence of this error, one day in 1955 a dozen unwitting female rats welcomed into their nests an equal number of protoplasmically morphed Axions, now indistinguishable from the rats' natural offspring. The Axion children soon recognized the mistake. Yet the bewildered changelings – led by the dashing Alyak – valiantly tried to carry on with the mission of making contact with the dominant species, which they now saw was the humans. The rest of the book was taken up with detailed descriptions of their gruesome deaths at the hands of this merciless species, even though the real rats, who still thought of the Axions as their own, made noble and self-sacrificing attempts to save them. Each time an Axion was murdered on Earth, exact imagery of his death was transmitted telepathically across the galaxy to Axi 12, and so horrible were the pictures that they roused even the peaceful and ethically superior Axion public to fury. Though it took their spaceships a few years to reach Earth, when they got there they turned it into a fireball. Hence the burning cities on the cover. In the epilogue, set in 1985, all humans have perished, along with all other large carnivores, while on the charred crust of the ruined planet, the Norway rat rules unchallenged.

I closed *The Nesting* and sat on it. I was on the verge of tears, and next to Jerry's name I posted the words SOUL MATE and SOLITUDE. I understood now that he needed the big wire basket on the front of his bicycle just to cart around his enormous despair and that the eye that looked off to the side was staring out at the blank nothingness of human life and the infinity of time and space, a nothingness and an infinity that he had brought together in his book under the name of the Great Empty. And you can imagine the sort of boost the novel gave to my own self-esteem. No more damp spots in the jungle, no more meaningless words and gestures – I had a whole new story. To the labels of PERVERT, FREAK, and UNNATURAL GENIUS, I could now append the justificatory adjective EXTRA-TERRESTRIAL. It helps a lot, on lonely nights, to be able to look up at the stars and see them not as flakes of burning ice in the Great Empty but as the window lights of home. Unfortunately, being an extraterrestrial does not confer any of the practical advantages of wealth or fame, nor does it at all increase the likelihood of your getting through the day without some calamity falling on your head. And besides, I never really believed the story.

During business hours, when I was not asleep or hanging out of the Balloon, you could find me on the Balcony. Nothing that happened in the store below escaped my scrutiny. When Norman made an especially big sale, ringing it up on the ornate antique cash register that stood on a stand by the door, I clapped my paws and silently shouted, 'Way to go, Norm!' *Cheers from the Sidelines of Life.*

Pembroke Books was a big store – four rooms full of books, not counting the basement – and Norm knew it like the back of his hand. But even he was fallible. Occasionally he sought and did not find, stabbed and came up empty. When this happened, it was painful to watch. I remember one time in particular. The quarry was the slim *Ballad of the Sad Café*. The pursuer was a dwarf, a young woman dressed in a camel's-hair coat so large it hung around her like a tepee and dragged on the ground. The bottom edge was rimmed with mud. She had been hanging around for a while, apparently browsing, but I think really just working up the courage to speak. As soon as she had voiced her request – if *voiced* is the word for her blushing whisper – Norman had spun on his heels and strode confidently back to the shelves of paperback novels, his arm outstretched before him, his thick fingers curling in anticipation. You could almost imagine the book jumping off the shelf into his hand. But this time, you would imagine in vain. This time, the vast cerebral file-and-retrieve system failed to perform. You could almost

hear the clunking sound in Norman's head as the apparatus malfunctioned. No book leaped, no fingers grasped. I watched with growing anxiety as he searched up and down the shelf where it was supposed to be, tapping the rows of books nervously with his forefinger as if counting them, and then ransacking the shelves above and below, his gestures ratcheting from smoothly confident to convulsive and distraught. When finally it was clear to everyone that the book was simply not there, obviously not there, painfully not there, his manly shoulders sagged in defeat.

'Well, I thought we had it, but it seems I was mistaken. I am truly sorry.'

He said this to the floor just in front of his feet, unable to look the disappointed customer in the eye. He looked awfully upset, and I could tell he had upset the dwarf as well, who no doubt regretted she had ever asked. Oh, how I longed then to leap from my hiding place, to call out, 'Here it is, Mr Shine' – I would be careful to call him 'Mr Shine' to his face – 'I have it over here – it got slipped in with the cookbooks.' Astonished, he would stammer, 'B-but how did *you* know that?' And I would say, 'Pembroke Books is more than just a business to me, sir – it is my home.' He would be terrifically impressed, and also moved. And that would be just the beginning. In my dream he took me on as an apprentice. I rapidly 'rose through the ranks' to chief clerk. I wore a green eyeshade. I loved the way I looked in that eyeshade, sitting at the front desk late at night, catching up on paperwork – I reminded myself of Jimmy Stewart in *It's a Wonderful Life.*

The news from out in the world was bad. According to the *Globe*, General Logue had submitted his final battle plans to the city council. Lawyers for a couple of doomed families west of the Square were fighting on, but their cause was considered hopeless. And in June, the council gave its approval: in a matter of months the destruction would begin. Acres of heavy machinery stood on the outskirts, oiled and waiting. Every night or so after the council's decision another building burned as landlords struggled to cut their losses. The nights were laced with sirens, and sometimes the smoke was so thick it was hard to breathe in the streets. I kept working on my 'Ode to Night.' I thought of it as 'His Famous "Ode to Night."' Yet even with the store on its deathbed Norman kept on buying books. I guess he was like a shark too, worried about drowning.

I was always the dreamy type. And given my situation, what else could I be? But I also knew how to put four feet on the ground when I had to. And then – drenched, so to speak, by the drizzle of the real – I felt bad that in practice I could do nothing to help old Norman out. *Feelings of Inadequacy and the Origin of Depression in Males*. So I began to bring home little gifts. One night while scavenging popcorn on the floor of the Rialto, I found a gold ring. It was in the form of two intertwined serpents. At the top of the ring the opposite-facing heads lay side by side. They had tiny emeralds for eyes. Though I could have put the ring in a place where it would be found by the cleaning ladies, I did not do that. In fact, I stole it without the slightest twinge of conscience. I had long before discovered on my cranium a longish lump, almost a ridge, which according to Hans Fuchs – the man who first made use of Gall's science for practical police work – is a sure sign of 'criminal proclivities' and 'moral degeneration.' In fact, except for an obvious disqualification, I fit perfectly into Fuchs's category of *monstrum humanum*, the lowest order of criminal types. I knew there was no point in putting my conscience up to a battle it was bound to lose. As I said, I can be quite practical when I have to be. So I carried the ring home and placed it on Norman's desk next to his coffee mug, and there he found it the next morning. Clasping it with thumb and forefinger, he studied it a long time, he even tried it on, holding his hand out in front of him and turning it from side to side like a woman. Then he put it in a desk drawer. I figured he would think a customer must have lost it and I expected him to tack up a paper saying RING FOUND – CONTACT MANAGEMENT. He did not do that, though, and a week later I noticed the ring on his finger.

Another time, when I was skulking home from the Rialto just before dawn, I came across a man and a girl having some sort of dispute on Cambridge Street, which was deserted except for them. She was really going at him, shouting 'You fucker, you goddamn fucker' over and over, and each time she said 'fucker' she stamped her foot, as if keeping count of how many times she could say 'fucker' in a row. The man was swaying and trying to hold her by the shoulders but she kept shaking him off. He seemed really loaded, the way he was swaying. She had on silver shoes with very high heels, which reminded me of my Lovelies and made me feel sorry for her. Mentally, I was on her side, for what that was worth. In fact it was worth exactly nothing – why should a pretty girl like her give a shit that some scroungy little rat was on her side? She was holding a big bouquet of yellow roses in her hand, and at the end of perhaps the fifteenth 'fucker' she slapped him right across the face with the flowers, which went flying everywhere, and then she ran across the street and down into the subway. I shouted silently, 'Take that, you weasel!' The man just stood there a while, swaying slightly as if to a gentle breeze, among all those scattered roses like yellow flames on the sidewalk. Then he started stepping on them, pushing them down against the pavement with a twisting motion of the toe of his shoe. This was mirrored by a nearly identical twisting motion of his mouth. She stamps, he twists. He didn't miss even one. And then he walked slowly away down the street. I waited to make sure that he was not coming back, then I crept out and grabbed one of the roses, the one that seemed least damaged, and carried it home, where I straightened it out as best I could. It was almost opening time when I finally got it into the empty coffee mug on Norman's desk. I would have liked to put water in too but I had no way of doing that.

When I saw Norman's reaction to the flower, it occurred to me that I might have gone too far. He seemed frankly spooked. He stared at the strange yellow rose in his coffee cup, his eyes widening, and then he looked all around, even under the desk, as if worried somebody was about to jump out at him. He took the rose out of the mug and laid it on the desk. He kept shooting glances at it during the morning, as if he expected it suddenly to do something to explain its presence, and then after lunch he tossed it in the trash can. My gift had backfired. Instead of comfort, I had handed Norman just one more thing to worry about, and I was sorry. I didn't bring him any more presents after that.

I have never been right in the head, but I am not demented. You may raise an eyebrow here, you may raise both eyebrows, but the fact remains, daydreams and mental tricks are one thing, nuts is another. And I am not the kind of creature who can be crazy without knowing it. There are many people who are much worse off than I am. I have this from no less an authority that Peter Erdman, author of *The Self as Other*. In that book Dr Erdman recounts true tales of enormously fat people who can stand in front of a mirror and see an image of themselves no thicker than a Paris mannequin, and others, emaciated, who look in the mirror and see fat bulging like jelly rolls. They actually *see* this. Now that's crazy. With me, the problem has never been in the mirror – no one ever lives there but the same chinless fellow – but in the image of myself away from the mirror, the one I see when I lie on my back and look at my toes and tell myself all the wonderful stories, when I engage in what I call dreaming, taking the senseless stuff of life and giving it a beginning, middle, and end. My dreams contain everything – everything, that is, except the monster in the mirror. When I dream a sentence like 'The music died away, and in the silence all eyes were on Firmin, who stood aloof and unflinching in the doorway of the ballroom,' I never see an undersized chinless rat in the doorway of the ballroom. That would have a very different effect. No, I always see someone looking very much like Fred Astaire: thin waist, long legs, and a chin like the toe of a boot. Sometimes I even dress like Fred Astaire. In this particular scene I am in tails and spats and top hat. Legs crossed at the ankles, I am leaning casually on a silver-pommeled cane. Do you find it difficult to hold your eyebrows in that position? Sometimes, when I drop in for a cup of coffee with Norman, I am wearing a tan cardigan and tassel loafers. I lean back in my chair, throw my feet up on the desk, and we talk books and women and baseball. Next to that picture I have posted the phrase A GREAT CONVERSATIONALIST. And sometimes, still looking a lot like Astaire – but now dissipated, world-weary, a Lucky Strike hanging from my lip, like a Frenchman – I am pounding away with desperate fury at an old Remington. I love the sound the carriage makes when I tear out one page and furiously crank in the next. I could go on and on, tell you about the knock on the door, the way Ginger comes in, shy, carrying a cheese sandwich she has made for me, the look in her eyes. I could even tell you what is written on the pages that are piling up next to the typewriter.

There is a passage in *The Phantom of the Opera* where

the phantom, a great genius who lives hidden from sight because of his great ugliness, says that the thing he wants most in the world is simply to stroll in the evening along the boulevards with a beautiful woman on his arm, like an ordinary bourgeois. To me that is one of the most moving passages in literature, even though Gaston Leroux was not a Big One.

Chapter 7

Every week the paper brought more depressing news about the so-called renovation of Scollay Square. Many local businesses had already closed, following enormous going-out-of-business sales, and now stood dark and empty behind plywood sheeting, while others had simply burned to the ground. Even so, Norman kept at it. And we still had good days, though none like the old days. Fewer customers even on the best days, and on rainy days Norman did not even bother hauling out the feather duster. I occasionally saw customers blowing the dust off the books before they opened them, but he seemed never to notice. He slogged on, but you could tell his heart was not in it.

I slogged on too. With business down I had more time to work on dream structures. They were enormous dreams, like novels. I sometimes spent days on a single scene. Maybe it was a picnic at Revere Beach. Maybe it was the summer of 1929, and the stock market is about to crash and nobody knows it. What are they wearing? What kind of shoes? What sort of underpants? How do they cut their hair? What does the car look like? What do the seats feel like? How much does gas cost? Have they brought along a book? What are the sandwiches made of? What are they wrapped in? What brand of cigarette? Of soda? What kind of bird is that singing? What is that tree it is hiding in? All this would be a fairly easy assignment for me now. I have dreamed my way into things as far away as Tang China, Machu Picchu, and the seventy-third floor of the Empire State Building.

Late one night, I was busy with my mad French poet dream. I – or he or Fred Astaire, it doesn't matter – had lost a leg fighting on the side of the Paris Commune. Years of pain and absinthe had driven him – me, us – crazy. In the present scene, set on a rainy night, we see him in a narrow Paris street beating with a fist on the front door of a house belonging to the great actress Sarah Bernhardt. In his other hand he clutches, wrapped in oilcloth against the rain, fragments of his great mad poem 'Ode à la Nuit.' I was in the basement reading about Sarah Bernhardt in the *Encyclopedia Britannica*, when I was startled by the noise of the shop door opening. Diving into the ancestral hole, I scrambled up ink black shafts and reached the Balcony just as Norman was hanging up his raincoat. So it was raining in Boston too. He had never before returned to the shop after closing, and I followed him with worried eyes as he walked from aisle to aisle, looking all about him as if this were the first time he had ever been there. Then he sat down in his usual chair. He sat on the familiar red cushion, placed both hands flat on the desk, and began to cry. He did not make any sound, did not cover his face, the tears just ran silently out, mixing with the raindrops on his cheeks and chin and falling on his shirt. Silently I called out, 'Courage, Mr Shine. Tomorrow's another day. Don't do anything foolish.' I felt so bad that all I could think of were clichés. I even considered pitching myself headfirst from the Balloon just to distract him.

But what I really wanted to do, what in fact I almost did, was to rush out of the Rathole, throw myself at his feet, and madly kiss his shoe. He would be deeply touched. He would take me with him when he moved. It is interesting the way illusions have no end. What would Norman really think if a rat rushed from behind a safe and attached itself to his shoe? In the real world there are differences that cannot be bridged.

Life is short, but still it is possible to learn a few things before you pop off. One of the things I have observed is how extremes coalesce. Great love becomes great hatred, quiet peace turns into noisy war, vast boredom breeds huge excitement. It was the same with Norman and me. I would say that that night in the shop when Norman wept and I floated, almost weeping, overhead, was the high point of our relationship, our moment of maximum closeness. Great intimacy spawns huge estrangement. That was a Saturday night. The shop was always closed on Sunday so I did not see anything of Norman the next day. Sunday night I came back from the Rialto feeling sick. Bad wiener, probably. This had happened before, and I was not worried. And though I felt better Monday morning, I was still a little seedy, so I decided not to risk a run to the Rialto the following night even though that would mean no food before the run on Tuesday.

Norman was back at his desk with newspaper and coffee, and I was in the Balloon, alert for signs of distress. I watched him closely as he very slowly lowered his coffee cup, so slowly he barely rippled his right eye and cheek floating like lily pads on the brown water. I wondered, was this strangely retarded motion another symptom of grief? Because of my aversion to mirrors, I had never quite gotten the hang of the rules of refraction. So I did not immediately grasp that if I could see his eye, then he could see mine. Oblivious to the implications of that fatal symmetry, I continued to lean out over the edge of the Balloon while Norman pushed slowly back in his chair, hands clasped behind his head as if stretching. He was now looking straight up at the ceiling, and for a long moment his gaze, dark and somber, mingled with mine, black and glittering. *Terror and Recognition*. Then I jerked my head back and retreated into the darkness between the joists, where I crouched in a tumult of fear and delight. *He had seen me!* What would he do now? I was no longer alone. I tried to recall his eyes. What were they saying? In retrospect I imagined I had seen love there. Intelligent, kind Norman, of course he had been able to overlook the vanishing chin, the hairy cheeks, of course he had been able to see past the glittering eyes and into the soul of a fellow artist and businessman.

I passed the rest of that day deep in hiding. Only when I had heard the shop door close and lock and Norman's footsteps fade away down the sidewalk did I creep up to the Balcony to take a look around. Back in April I had carried loads of shredded paper up from the old familial nest into the Balcony and with it I had humped up a little fauteuil. It had been pleasant to sit there and watch what was going on in the store below. Sometimes I had stayed on up there after closing time, dreaming away, while the yellowing evening slowly filled the shop with a kind of airy grief. I loved the deepening shadows and the sadness that always overtook me then. But on the evening in question I saw right away that while I, quivering with fear and hope, had been holed up between the joists, Norman had paid a covert visit there. The fauteuil had been shoved aside and pretty much wrecked, and next to it lay a little heap of strange food. A little pile of cylindrical neon green pellets. They smelled good, so I nibbled. They were oddly delicious, tasting like a blend of Velveeta cheese, hot asphalt, and Proust. I recalled the look in Norman's eyes at the moment when they had met mine, and I thought, So it was love after all. And in that way began – and briefly endured – one of the happiest moments of my life. I was sure now that I was not alone. I *belonged* to someone. I nibbled again. In all my months of scrounging, the Rialto had never delivered up a food like this one. It was smooth like gumdrops, crunchy like popcorn, and had, as I mentioned, a flavor at once delicious and odd. I tried to imagine a name and settled on Normans, as in 'A box of Normans, please.' It made me sad that I was still too queasy from wiener poisoning to eat more than a few of the nicely bite-sized pieces.

Afterward I fell asleep right there on the Balcony. I dreamed I was dancing with Norman. I was dressed in

one of Ginger Rogers's silk gowns and he was wearing in his lapel the yellow rose I had given him. He was feeding me Normans with his fingers while we danced, pushing them one at a time into my mouth, pushing in one for each downbeat of the music. This was pleasant at first, but then, when he would not stop even after I was gagging but kept on forcing them in, it turned nightmarish. I woke up coughing and full of anguish. I tried to vomit but couldn't.

The next morning I felt worse. I was dizzy and had a painful cough, and there was a roaring in my ears like rushing water. I went back and ate some more of the new food and felt a little better. But that evening I was worse again and so weak that taking even a few slow steps was like climbing a mountain. I had not had anything to drink for two days, and now all I could think about was water. I saw, looking down from the Balloon, that Norman had not rinsed his cup. Half an inch of brown liquid languished at the bottom. I decided to go get it, and I half climbed, half fell down the central shaft to the Rathole. When I reached the floor, I discovered that the hole had been partially blocked by a small cardboard box. It took all my strength to push it away from the opening. It was heavy because it was filled almost to the top with Normans. I was climbing over it to get out of the hole when I caught sight of the label. It said 'RatOut.' It also said, as subtext, 'Normans, my ass.' It did *not* say 'delicious and wholesome snack.' It *did* say 'kills in one feeding.' I wondered if the half-dozen pellets I had swallowed would count as one feeding. I read on: 'For control of mice, Norway rats, and roof rats in homes, farms, and businesses.' I was not sure if I was Norway or roof, though it apparently did not matter. 'Keep out of reach of children and pets.' Cruel words to one who had briefly imagined that he might be both. I was dying, like Peewee, but slower, and not killed accidentally, but murdered. I made it to the coffee and drank it, and then I spent over an hour crawling back up to the nest. Even lying down I could not get my breath. I kept coughing, and when I wasn't coughing my lungs made a wheezing sound like someone screaming from the bottom of a deep hole. When I sucked on my gums, I could taste the blood. I imagined myself dying. Fred Astaire, the great dancer, dying. John Keats, the great poet, dying. Apollinaire, delirious, dying. Proust, beautiful eyes in shrunken face, dying. Joyce dying in Zurich. Stevenson dying in Samoa. Marlowe dying, murdered. I was sorry no one was going to be there to see it. The beautiful butterflies were going to fold their wings and I was going to die like any other rat.

I slept a long time. And when I woke I was not in heaven, unless heaven is a dusty place between two wooden joists. I still felt very weak but could not suck blood from my gums anymore. I was terribly thirsty and hungry as a wolf. The light from below streaming up around the edge of the Balloon was filled with dancing motes. Watching them, I was moved almost to tears by the beauty of it all. I crawled a few steps, and the feeling of the roughness of the laths against my feet was inexpressibly sweet. I crawled to the edge of the Balloon and looked down. He was sitting at the desk reading the paper as if nothing had happened. Looking down at his bald pate, I now had no trouble guessing at what sinister bumps he cunningly concealed beneath that monkish wreath of curly hair. I could easily have loosened the light fixture and sent it crashing down on his unprotected skull. Odd as it may seem, while such a thought did cross my mind, it found no purchase there. Throughout my life an enormous fatalism has always protected me from feelings of bitterness and rancor. And besides, it would be revenge on a phantom, since the Norman I had known and loved had turned out not to exist at all, to be in fact just a figment of my imagination, the product of an enormous misunderstanding for which I alone was to blame. He had turned out to be just another character in my dreams, with no more substance than the mad poet who the week before had been beating on Sarah Bernhardt's door. I was heartbroken. *Rat Poison, or a Love Betrayed.* Everything I had thought fixed and firm had come unglued, and yet at the same time I felt reborn. I was ready, as they say, to turn the page. With Pembroke Books on the short path to oblivion and with its owner a murderer, bearing on his temples the mark of Cain, it was time to make plans.

Chapter 8

There are two kinds of animals in the world, those with the gift of language and those without. Animals with the gift of language in turn fall into two classes, the talkers and the listeners. Most of the latter are dogs. Dogs, however, being exceedingly stupid, bear their aphasia with a kind of servile joy, which they express by wagging. That was not the case with me – I could not stand the thought that I would pass all my days in silence.

Long ago, when I was just beginning my love affair with humans, I had come across in my reading various ingenious devices designed to mitigate that species' natural inclination to malfunction and decay: prosthetic limbs, dentures, trusses, hearing aids, and eyeglasses. And so I early on hatched the idea of supplementing my natural deficiency with some sort of mechanical apparatus. When I first encountered the word *typewriter*, it was without explanation, as something obvious and familiar, and I was able to glean only that it was a thing with keys over which the nimble fingers of women sometimes flew. At first I thought it must be a kind of musical instrument and was puzzled by its connection with *clatter*. When I finally figured out that it was a machine for putting words on paper, I was tremendously excited. Though there was no typewriter anywhere that I could put my paws on, just the idea of it loosed a flood of images. I saw myself planting brilliant typewritten notes around the shop for Norman to find and puzzle over. In my dreams, he found them and scratched his head and left little missives in reply.

Well, we already know how Norman let me down. The typewriter ditto. I dug up detailed descriptions and labeled drawings, and I even saw them at work in the movies. The verdict was unequivocal: too big, too heavy. When you are small, it is not enough to be a genius. Even if I could depress the keys, perhaps by jumping on them from a height, I would never be able to wind paper into the roller – rats are not good at knobs – or work the long silver lever that made the carriage rasp back into place. I had learned from the movies that a typewriter really does make a kind of music, and I knew that I was never going to hear it for myself, the bright *ping* of accomplishment at the end of a line or the long applauding scrape of the carriage slamming back to start another. As things have turned out, when I finish a line I hear nothing, just the silence of thoughts falling endlessly down the hole of memory.

But as I have said before, I can be very persistent when I want something badly enough, and I did not give up on the idea of conversing with humans. Only a couple of weeks after abandoning the typewriter project, I had discovered under LANGUAGES a slim yellow pamphlet called *Say It Without Sound: A Pictionary*, and there I found pictures of dozens of the signs used by the deaf to speak. When I first came across this book I was sure that at last I had found what I sought. Common words were arranged alphabetically, as in a dictionary, and opposite each entry as its 'definition' was a photo of a pretty woman in a red sweater making the corresponding sign. It was because of her, I suppose, that the idea of signing became associated with Lovelies. Next to the word *friend*, for example, was a picture of the shapely-sweatered Lovely holding her left and right index fingers together. Friendly fingers close together. So I got my hopes up again. Foolishly, it turned out, since I soon discovered that whoever had devised this silent language had intended it for creatures equipped with fingers. With what I had in the way of feet and claws, I found it impossible to stammer out even the most rudimentary phrases. I could manage at best a kind of digital stutter. I stood in front of the mirror, painful as that was, and balancing on the rim of the sink, struggled to say in sign, 'What do you like to read?' I tried letting my body stand for a palm and my legs for fingers and then midway through the phrase changed the principle and let my forelegs stand for arms and my hind legs for thumbs. Slapping my chest now, then crossing my legs, then curling up in a ball, I flung myself frantically about like a man with his clothes on fire. It was useless.

Desperate situations, however, breed desperate hopes, and so after being nearly poisoned to death by Shine I went back to the idea of signing. At this point I figured a rudimentary phrase might be all I needed, just something to let people know that I was smart and

friendly. It had been a long time since my first attempts, and though few things left the store without my knowledge, I was apprehensive that someone might have slipped out with the pamphlet one day when I was away at the Rialto or ratnapping in the ceiling. Someone deaf, of course, and therefore very silent. So as soon as Shine had locked the door that night and coughed once (a habit he had, a kind of hello to the evening), and carried his footfalls down the street, I tumbled to the ground floor and tore across the shop to the corner where the book used to be. And where it was still: a yellow slice sandwiched like cheese between the dark pumpernickel of a Serbo-Croatian dictionary and the paler rye of Langston's *Fundamentals of Business German*. When with great effort I had contrived to dislodge it from the shelf, I noticed that the price penciled on the inside cover had shriveled from twenty-five cents to a nickel.

Turning the pages slowly, I questioned the Lovely. I was looking for the simplest and most intelligible phrase permitted by my physiological limitations, and in no time at all I had learned to say 'good-bye zipper.' It wasn't Shakespeare, but it was the best I could manage. I was able to say this by standing on my hind legs and waving a forepaw – waving good-bye – followed by a zipping motion up my chest with the same paw. I practiced in front of the mirror, wave-zip, wave-zip, until I had it down pat – which brought me face-to-face with a new problem: who was I going to say this to? Obvious answer: a deaf person. Which at least gave me a new goal in life: find a deaf person.

Deaf people, however, do not grow on trees. I kept my eyes open, hoping one would just happen to walk into the store, in which case I planned to rush out and introduce myself. I don't think any ever did, though one day an old man came in and spent a long time browsing and finally picked out a book and paid for it without saying a word. So he might have been deaf. But with Shine around I figured I could not take any chances. The man was old and frail, and had I rushed out and thrown myself at his feet, he might not have been able to protect me.

I had never physically traveled outside of Scollay Square, but I knew a lot about Boston from books and maps and could see it all in my head stretched out below me, Arlington to Columbus Point, as from an airplane. Now, like a true Axion, my task was to make contact with the dominant species. I had of course already tried that with Shine and had nearly met an Axion's fate. But wide reading had left no doubt in my mind that in addition to crowds of sadists, fiends, psychopaths, and poisoners, the dominant species also sported exemplars of gentleness and compassion, and that most of the latter were women. I could have sought contact in the streets of the Square, but something in the faces there warned me not to. I have already confessed that at the time I was still very bourgeois, and consequently I wanted as my first interlocutor, as, so to speak, my virginal partner in human converse, what I then thought of as a superior class of person. With the most likely spots for that sort of superior female person – the campuses of Wellesley and Radcliffe and the Saint Claire Nunnery in Jamaica Plain – out of reach, I fell back on the Public Garden, just a few blocks west of the Square. And in this you see again that despite a tendency to pickiness I have all four feet on the ground and can be quite practical when I have to.

I needed a rainy night for travel, when people would be too busy clinging to the newspapers and umbrellas above their heads as they dashed between cars and doorways to notice a small, low animal creeping its way westward beneath the parked vehicles. I did not have to wait long. The following Saturday, Shine left the shop at five o'clock under the dripping dome of a black umbrella. And sometime after midnight, when I set out for the Public Garden, the rain was coming down hard, though the asphalt beneath the cars was still dry and warm. Only the intersections presented problems, open spaces to be crossed at a sprint. I bided my time at those places – I had not forgotten poor Peewee – and it was nearly dawn when I finally crossed the Common and made my final dash into the Public Garden.

The grass there was soft and smelled good and sweet. It was my first grass, and I ate some. The rain had stopped, and the sky was paling in the east. After crawling under parked cars, from car to car all the way up Tremont Street, my legs and the underparts of my body were black and matted with grit and oil. I cleaned myself as best I could, then crept under some bushes and slept. When I woke, the sun was shining, and I saw the trees. I had never seen real trees before. The bush

I was hiding under was near a concrete path that ran all the way across the Public Garden. I looked out and saw people in nice clothes walking. Church bells were ringing. I had a strange detached feeling, as if I were seeing myself from above. A rat that should be dead was not dead. Weak and dirty but in no way dead, he was alive under a bush, and he had a plan.

I watched the people walking, watched what they did with their hands. Were their hands talking? All morning I watched hands swing by sides, hide in pockets, pat down wind-ruffled hair, wave hello, point at squirrels, make fists, toss peanuts, pick noses, scratch crotches, and hold other hands. The hands all went busily about these affairs without ever speaking. I ate grass. Twice I darted out and pinched peanuts meant for squirrels. It was not enough. I had not eaten a real meal for over a day. I was feeling weak, and the weakness made me afraid.

It was nearly dark when I saw them coming, two women and a little girl between them, walking up from Arlington Street. They were wearing nice clothes and had shiny shoes. Above the girl's head the women's hands were talking. I was sorry that I had not spent more time studying the pictionary so that I could understand what the hands were saying. My heart was pounding. I worried about my weakness, that in my fear and excitement I was going to faint. I watched as they came closer, and when they were close I rushed out into the middle of the walk, and my paws said 'good-bye zipper.' I tried to shout it by making my gestures as violent as possible. Good-bye zipper. Good-bye zipper. Absurdly, I tried to heighten the effect by squeaking as loud as I could. I could tell that I was getting through. The women and the girl had stopped and all three were staring open-mouthed. Good-bye zipper. I had to stand on my hind legs to say this, and in my enthusiasm I lost my balance and fell over backward. One of the women started making a breathy grunting sound, huh huh huh, she might have been laughing, and then the little girl screamed. I am not clear on the exact progression of events after that. Some people were shouting 'Rat, rat!' A man's voice said, 'Of course it's not a squirrel,' and another voice said, 'It's having a fit,' and a third said, 'Rabies,' and then they all were talking at once. A man came with a walking stick and tried to poke me in the stomach. I was back on my feet and running, and the man tried to strike me with the stick. I heard it crack against the pavement, and then it went up in the air and whooshed and came down on my back just as I made the grass edge, and someone shouted, 'Don't hurt it.' I got into the row of bushes and ran. I did not feel any pain but I knew that I was dragging something heavy behind me. I turned my head and saw that my left leg was twisted the wrong way. It did not move as I ran, and I dragged it behind me like a sack.

The pain came in the night, and by the next morning I could barely haul myself forward using only my front legs, the pain was so huge. I ate grass. From my hiding place I watched a man feed squirrels. He was sitting on a bench near me with a paper sack in his lap, and the squirrels climbed up and took peanuts from between his fingers. *Greed and Degradation among America's Wildlife*. After a while he seemed to get bored. He turned the sack upside down and all the peanuts spilled out on the bench and on the ground. The man walked off and the squirrels rushed around snatching up peanuts, and when they thought there weren't any more they left too. But they had missed one peanut, I could see it in the grass against the foot of the bench just a few feet from where I was hiding. Someone else came and sat on the bench, someone blue. I didn't care. I wanted the peanut too much to care about anything but that, and I crawled out and got it. I remember how good it tasted.

Chapter 9

The next things I recall are a swaying motion and a strong human smell. When I came to I found myself swaddled like a papoose in human smell and suffocating layers of wool cloth. It was dark in there, and swaying, and full of pain. Clawing at the folds of rough cloth with my forefeet, I managed to work my head out into the fresh air. Gasping great mouthfuls of it, I saw a blue sky hatched by wires, edged by the tops of buildings. I pulled back another fold, folded it down, and I could see the cars that we were passing on one side, that were passing us on the other. Twisting my head back I looked into the sky straight above, and then, farther back, into a human eye of the same clear blue. It was looking straight at me, while its mate watched the traffic.

Jerry Magoon was breathing hard with the effort of pedaling and his breath was blowing his mustache out each time he exhaled. The bike swayed from side to side as he pedaled, and the wire basket rocked like a cradle. I rested my head on the redolent wool, which I later learned was Jerry's sweater, Jerry's smell, and closed my eyes. The thick cloth of the sweater dulled the jolts of the road but did not stop the pain in my leg. Beneath the basket the front wheel squeaked. I would have liked to tell Jerry good-bye zipper, but I did not have the strength, and anyway I doubted he would understand.

And that was how I came to Cornhill the second time. I had ridden in first on the swaying waters of Mama's womb, and now in the folds of Jerry's sweater. Like Moses, I rode in in a basket.

When we got to Pembroke Books, Jerry lifted the bike over the curb as gently as he could and leaned it against the shop window. Shine's scowl flew at us through the glass – his wide face looked like an owl swooping at us through the window. Peering up from my woolly covert in the basket, I was closer to him than I had ever been before, closer even than on that fateful day when our eyes had first met, mine full of love and his full of . . . what? Looking back, I suppose it was contempt.

Jerry just ignored him as usual.

He cradled me in an armful of wool, and we went into the doorway under ROOMS. Using his elbows he pushed open the door that said DR LIEBERMAN PAINLESS DENTIST on the glass. It closed behind us with a sigh. It was darker inside, with a cold wet smell. Heavily and slowly, placing first his right foot on a tread and then bringing his left up to stand beside it, like a child, he carried me up three flights of dark stairs. His mustache rose and fell with his breathing, and we rested a while on the landings. There were several doors on each floor. All were painted brown except Dr Lieberman's, which was green, and each had a frosted glass transom above it.

Jerry's room was on the top floor at the back. Shifting the sweater onto a crooked elbow, he dug in his pocket. He excavated a handful of stuff – a book of matches, coins, a piece of white string, some peanuts, a brass screw. Spilling most of it onto the floor, he managed to extract a key. His fingers were short and thick. He unlocked the door, nudging it open with his foot, and we went in. He put me carefully down on the bed, easing his arm out from under the wool so as not to jostle, and arranged the sweater into a kind of nest around me. Then he pushed it down on one side so I could see over without lifting my head.

The room was not very big, and at first glance its primary function seemed to be storage. Besides the furniture – an iron bedstead, a leather armchair split and spilling white stuffing, a chest of drawers surmounted by a tilting mirror on which someone had drawn, in lipstick perhaps, a walleyed mustachioed face sticking its tongue out, bookshelves constructed of unpainted boards and concrete blocks, a table with a white enamel top chipped black along the edges – there were boxes, cardboard cartons and wooden crates, piled one on top of the other almost to the ceiling. Precariously on top of the tallest stack teetered a child's red wagon, the kind that is pulled by a long metal handle. The sides of this wagon had been extended by the addition of wooden planks on which someone had painted by hand E. J. MAGOON in big red and yellow letters, as on a circus wagon. A few minutes later Jerry brought up his bicycle and wedged it in with all the rest. I have never seen a human live so much like a rat.

He opened a door next to the bookshelves and rummaged in a closet, digging with his arms and grunting and throwing things out on the floor behind him – clothes, boots, a partially demolished record player, a toaster, a lot of *Life* magazines, and more boxes. He reminded me of a dog digging in the dirt. On the other side of the bookshelves from the closet was a kind of alcove with a sink and a counter. A blue cloth hung from the counter to the floor, concealing, I later learned, a metal garbage can. On top of the counter, amid a litter of pans and plates, was a green Coleman camp stove. Daylight struggled through the greasy panes of a single large window. This had a pull shade but no curtains, and beneath it was a radiator that someone had tried – with only partial success – to paint red.

Jerry found what he was looking for in the closet: a gray Florsheim shoe box, which he upended over the bed, spilling the contents out in a pile next to where I lay – letters, envelopes, a handful of blue and white playing cards with BICYCLE on the back, and lots of photographs. In one I saw upside down a much younger Jerry with short black hair and a long upper lip like Henry Miller's. He was sitting at a table covered with papers. Interrupted at his writing, still holding a pen to the page, he was looking up and smiling stiffly. He had white teeth. The old gray one smiled too and spoke to me softly and told me not to worry or be frightened, and his mustache moved while the words crept out beneath it. His teeth were long and yellow now and his breath smelled like cigarettes and meat.

He placed a folded towel – it said ROOSEVELT HOTEL – at the bottom of the box and gently lifted me in and put the box on the floor. The towel had blue stripes on it. It did not smell of Jerry. He kept talking to me in that soft cheerful voice – deep and full of gravel – while he poked around in the refrigerator without turning his head.

'What's yours, Chief?' he graveled. 'Milk? . . . Milk's good.' He pulled out a jar with a red lid. 'Ever try peanut butter?' He knelt by my box, huge head bending over.

I never had tried peanut butter. Or milk, apart from the funny stuff I had scrounged from Mama. The milk came in a jar top and the peanut butter in a dollop on a piece of waxed paper. Peanut butter was the best thing I had ever tasted. It was named Skippy. And the milk too was good, so cool and sweet. He watched me eating. He watched me lap the milk, and he smiled. He said, 'Yum yum, drink 'em up.'

Then he fussed around in the alcove. He cooked rice in a pot of water, and when it was cooked he drained it by tipping the pot over the sink while holding the lid on with a toweled hand. A cloud of steam rose from the sink and misted the window. He looked at me and said 'Kavoom.' He laughed, shaking the gravel around in his lungs. He shook soy sauce on the rice and stirred it around. He pushed aside stacks of books and papers and dirty dishes to clear a spot for his plate at the table. He ate the rice with a spoon, holding the spoon in his fist like a child and chewing very slowly. I hoped he would talk to me some more, but he did not that night.

After dropping all the dishes in the sink – *kavoom* – he took his jacket and went out and was gone a long time, and when he came back it was so late the city was almost quiet except for now and then a siren or car horn and the loud throbbing in my leg, and he went to bed without turning on the light again. He smelled like Mama. I could hear him sleeping, slow and heavy, and heard him laugh in a dream, and in the morning I saw that he was still in his clothes.

And that was how I began my life with Jerry Magoon, the second human I ever loved. I was not able to move around much for a few days, and the pain would not let me sleep. I lay quietly in my box and named things. The table, which was always loaded down with stuff, I named the Camel. I called my box the Hotel. The window became La Fontaine Lumineuse, and I named the leather armchair Stanley. I named things and I watched Jerry. I followed with my eyes everything he did in the daytime, and in the night I listened to his breathing.

He had folded my towel in such a way that it said VELT on top, and when I lay down with one eye shut and the other pressed close to the towel and sighted across the rolling hills of its nappy surface, I could see a vast savanna stretching away before me, from the huge T in the foreground like a great leafless baobab, to the little V standing for 'vanishing' in the distance. During those first days, whenever Jerry went out, I would lie quietly and watch the gazelles leaping over and over the E and the giraffes scratching their knobby

heads on the L. I could do this for hours. And when, finally, I would hear Jerry's key rattle in the latch and lift my head from the towel, the poor frightened animals would fly off like birds, their muffled cries receding over the grassy plain. It was so sad and beautiful. I thought that in the end I would prefer being a gazelle leaping and floating over E to being human and that I would rather have long legs than a chin.

My leg healed fairly quickly, and by the end of a week I was able to put weight on it again. And after a few more days it hurt scarcely at all, though it stayed crooked, and I have hobbled ever since. *Hobble* is a nice word. It does what it says. I was never a sportive type, and I did not really mind being crippled. If anything, I felt it lent me a distinguished look. I would have liked to add a little cane and sunglasses. I have always felt close to the words *panache* and *debonair*. I would have liked to be able to grow a small black goatee.

Jerry called me Chief for a while, which I did not much like, then he tried out Gustav and Ben, and finally settled on Ernie. The importance of being Ernest. Ernest Hemingway. Ernie. He gave me all the peanut butter and milk I wanted, and he offered me bits of toast for breakfast and anything he was having that he thought I might enjoy, like rice, which he cooked, or creamed corn, which he got out of a can. We found out rats don't care for pickles.

He was away a lot, sometimes in the day and sometimes at night, sometimes to the public library in Copley Square and sometimes to Flood's Bar on the corner, but most of the time to places unknown. He always wore a dark blue suit when he went out. He had two suits just alike. He washed them himself in the sink and dried them on the fire escape or on the radiator, but he never ironed them. And he always wore a necktie, too, which he did not draw up tight. He never untied it – just slipped it on over his head and let it hang around his neck like a noose. He always looked as if he had just come off a binge, and if I had to summarize his appearance in a word it would be *rumpled.*

When I was able to climb out of the Hotel and limp around the room, Jerry did not object. He was a terrible housekeeper, and he did not object to anything I did, even pulling the stuffing out of Stanley, which I enjoyed doing, and getting down inside the springs, though I never tested him by snooping in his personal things while he was around. Once back on my feet, I took advantage of his long absences to sniff out every inch of the place, starting with the bookcase. I have never been in any other person's home, so I don't know how many books are usually in one. After Pembroke Books, of course, almost any number would seem small. I guess Jerry had about two hundred. I was happy to see *Portrait of the Artist* and *Ulysses*, though the Great Book was sadly missing – sadly, because I have never been able to recover the pages that Flo tore up and that I unwittingly ate. In addition to the books, the bottom shelf held a long row of notebooks of the kind Jerry did his writing in. Nosy as I normally am, I still did not feel it was right to snoop in these, though the temptation was awful. I did read his regular books, however – quite a number were new to me. I started at the bottom left and worked my way up, and it wasn't long before he caught me at it.

I had just discovered Terry Southern, and I had his novel *Candy* open on the floor. It was one of those glued paperbacks that are always trying to snap shut like clams, and I was holding it down with both forepaws. The story was very stimulating. I had gotten to the place where Candy is having sex with the dwarf, and I was so engrossed in it – seeing, as I could not fail to do, a certain similarity to my own situation – that I didn't hear Jerry coming up the stairs until it was too late. The door must not have been latched, for suddenly there he was on the threshold, breathing heavily, a bag of groceries in one hand, still holding the room key in the other. He gave me a real start. For his part, he was so surprised he just stood there for a moment without moving, pointing his key at me like a pistol. Since I had, so to speak, been nabbed with the goods, I figured I now had little choice but to try and bluff my way through. So I just turned the page and went on reading. I expected him to be angry at me for dragging the book out onto the floor, but instead he thought it was terribly funny. When he got over his shock, he actually laughed aloud, something he did not do very often, throwing a whole lot of gravel on the roof. After that I did not hesitate to pull out a book whenever I was bored, open it on the floor, and read it through right there in front of him. I don't think he ever caught on that I really was reading. I think he thought right up to the end that I was just pretending.

Chapter 10

Though a person might not guess it to look at him, Jerry was a very conscientious and parsimonious person when he was sober. He liked to fish old broken things out of the trash and fix them, toasters and record players and the like. Sometimes he could and sometimes he couldn't. If he couldn't, he would throw them back out, and if he could, he would jam them in with the rest of the stuff in the closet. He could spend half a day taking some contraption apart on the table, fussing around with pliers and screwdrivers and rolls of black tape, talking to himself the whole time – 'Now that wire must go over here, that's the thermostat, and that's the spring catch, O.K., and it's broken right there' – and then putting it all back together. His eyes were so bad he practically had to work with his nose against the table, and what with his bad eyes and his thick fingers he sometimes dropped some of the little parts on the floor. I loved it when he crawled around on all fours looking for them. He reminded me of a bear. I suppose I could have fetched them for him, but I never did. And it was funny too to see him bent over his work with his big walleye staring out to the side. He looked like a child caught doing something naughty. And then whenever he did manage to resuscitate some moribund gadget he was so happy he would bounce around the room chortling and chuckling to himself. *Repairing the World: A Mechanic's Struggle*. Seeing him like that made me want to put the word radiance next to him. The happiness just flew off him and filled the room and I could take big breaths of it myself. After he had four or five of these things stacked in the closet and fixed up as good as new, he would load them all up in the red wagon and haul them off somewhere. I later learned he gave them away to people in the streets.

One day about a month after I came to live with him, Jerry brought home a toy piano he had dug out of the trash. It was white and stood on three little legs and came with a little bench. It was in every way like a real piano except it did not have so many keys, and some of the ones it had did not work. They made no sound at all when he struck them, or only a dull unmusical *thunk*. After hammering out three or four of those *thunks*, he sat down at the Camel and took the whole thing apart. He fiddled with it and talked to it for hours, and in the end he got most of the keys to work. Afterward he spent a couple of hours with it on his lap in the armchair, picking out tunes with two fingers, 'Streets of Laredo' and 'Swanee River.' Then he put it down on the floor and let me play with it. I loved that piano, and he knew it and never did give it away. I played mostly Cole Porter and Gershwin. And sitting on the bench, swaying to the music, I looked exactly like Fred Astaire, and I sang like him too. Sure, I know that this was true only from a certain perspective, and that all Jerry heard was a high ratlike squeak. But he loved it just the same. The first time I played and sang for him he laughed till tears ran down his cheeks. I would have preferred something other than laughter, but I did not really mind.

Jerry was the first real writer I had ever known, and I have to confess that despite his kindness I was disappointed at first. As I have said, I was still very bourgeois, and his was not at all what I thought a real writer's life should be like. For one thing, it was lonelier than I had ever imagined. Well, not lonelier than I had ever imagined, and not lonelier than I had experienced for myself, but it was lonelier than I thought real writers were. Only three times did anyone knock on our door during all the months we were together. I had always imagined that a real writer – and myself writing in my dreams – would spend a lot of time lounging about in cafes having witty conversations with scintillating people and that sometimes he would bring home a beautiful girl with long dark hair and then throw her out the next morning so he could get back to work – 'Sorry, doll, I've got a book to write.' I imagined him locked in his room for days at a time, drinking quarts of whiskey from a Woolworth tumbler and pounding at his Underwood into the wee hours. He was never clean-shaven and never had a beard, always just a two-day stubble. A certain bitterness lurked in the corners of his mouth, and his sad eyes betrayed an ironic *je ne sais quoi*. Jerry remotely conformed only to the whiskey part. I didn't know where he went when he left me at night, but he never brought home any interesting people. All he brought home were matchbooks from Flood's Bar and Lounge two doors down. And he did not seem to have any friends, even boring ones. Unless, of course, you counted mere acquaintances like Shine and the people who knew him as a character on the street. Everybody in the neighborhood knew Jerry Magoon in that way. In that way he was almost famous.

He did not spend a lot of time actually writing either, if writing means physically putting words on paper – an hour a day at most. When he did write in the physical way, he sat at the enamel-topped table, the same place he sat to eat and to fix things. It was always piled with stuff – papers, books, dirty dishes, clothing, an umbrella usually, and bits and pieces of things he was taking apart or putting back together – and he would push these aside to clear a space in which to write. He wrote with a pencil in school notebooks, the kind with black-and-white marbled covers and a white rectangle in the middle with lines for Name and Subject. The name on the one he was writing in the whole time I lived with him was *The Last Big Deal*. It did not have a subject.

Jerry mumbled and hummed while he wrote. The hum was a high singsong and the mumble was just a mumble or maybe a drone. It sounded like someone saying prayers in a distant room – it carried an aura of meaning and yet it was impossible to make out a single word. He mumbled even when he was not sitting at the table writing. In fact, except when he was actually talking to someone in person, he mumbled all the

time. I thought he was probably writing his books in his head the way I do. This was to me an encouraging thought, and it was around that time that I really got serious about my own writing.

Sometimes Jerry did drink a little too much, and then when he came back home he would bang into the furniture getting into bed and fall asleep in his clothes. I would hear him get up in the night to take them off. He always got up in the night anyway to pee in the sink. And now and then he went on a real knockdown binge. These invariably came at the end of one of his blue periods – down periods that rolled around like clockwork – and they always seemed to do him a lot of good. I didn't mind the drinking – why should I, after all, given my own history? – but I hated the blue periods. All his buried despair, all the sadness and hopelessness that you found in his books, would float to the surface of his life, bubble up into his eyes and cover his face like a veil. During those periods he just sat in the big leather chair and studied the wall, practically catatonic.

He even stopped eating and, closer to home, stopped feeding me. That made me feel really apprehensive. And I felt useless too. As you have probably guessed by now, I am a pretty depressive character myself and know all about the seventeen kinds of despair, so even if I had been able to talk I could not have said anything that would have made him feel better. When someone is in despair and tells you how cold and unkind the world is and how much pointless suffering there is in life and how much loneliness, and you just happen to agree with him on every point, it puts you in an awkward position. These spells of his lasted a couple of days usually, and I never gave up trying to snap him out of them. I did all sorts of tricks to amuse him – sang, played boogie-woogie on the piano, pulled funny faces, did my epileptic rat act, everything that in better times would have called forth a pretty big guffaw – but he seemed never to notice. Then, regular as sunrise, after two or three days, he would suddenly get up from his chair, splash cold water on his face, put on his jacket and tie, and without a word walk out the door.

These sudden exits terrified me at first. I thought he was probably going to look for a tall building or maybe a bridge over icy water. Sometimes I pretended I was Ginger and went out looking for him. I always found him before it was too late, usually in some wharf-district dive, sitting alone in a booth watching the ice melt in his whiskey. Timidly I would tug at his sleeve. 'Come home, Jerry, please.' He would jerk his arm free and angrily turn away. 'Please, Jerry, come back home. I need you.' And in the end I always managed to persuade him. I loved the way everybody in the bar looked at me and Jerry and felt sad for us. In reality, of course, I just sat home and worried. He would be gone for one night, maybe two, and then he would come back home again looking really terrible and fall into bed and sleep a long time. And when he woke up, he would be his old self again. Psychologically speaking, drunkenness is a lot more useful than people think.

One morning a couple of days after I moved in, when I was still confined to the

Hotel, I was startled awake by a huge commotion. Poking my nose over the edge of the box, I was surprised to see Jerry with his arms around the big leather armchair. Panting and grunting, he was struggling to shove it through the open window. I thought at first that he was throwing old Stanley out, and I expected a tremendous crash from below. But in fact he was just pushing the chair out onto the metal fire escape, and once it was there he climbed out after it, clutching a cup of coffee in one hand and a *Life* magazine in the other. On the cover it said 'Survive Fallout.' It turned out he often sat out there in fine weather, reading the paper or napping. Sometimes he took his shirt off and sunbathed. He had a mat of gray curly hair on his chest that tapered down in a v to his navel, and on his left bicep he had a tattoo of a red rose with a scroll of pale blue writing beneath it, so faded you could not read it anymore. I think it said 'forever,' though it might have been 'clever' or 'roll over.' He called the fire escape with the chair on it a balcony, just the way I had, but all you could see from his balcony was the backs of some buildings, the alley below, and a lot of very bent-up garbage cans. And the sky, of course. The city had stopped replacing the bulbs in the streetlights and one by one they had gone out until the neighborhood had grown so dark that we could sit out on the balcony at night and see the stars. They were my first stars. Like Jerry's arm, they said 'forever.'

The armchair on the fire escape was also the cause of the first knock we got on the door. It was the fire people, a small man in a uniform and a big man in an open-collared white shirt. The big one had chest hair like Jerry's except that his was black. He told Jerry that the armchair was blocking an emergency exit. He called it a 'safety hazard.' Jerry argued a while, saying that if there was a fire he could jump over the chair, did they want to see him jump over the chair? They did not, and they were angry that he was arguing, and they told him just to take the fucking chair of the fire escape. So Jerry went and wrestled the chair back in, grumbling and growling like a bear. Two days later he put the chair back out. It was what he called fighting the system.

When my leg had finally healed I set about exploring in earnest, searching for an exit. Nice as it was, the room was still a kind of prison. And after a few weeks I had started to really miss the bookstore, the hum and bustle of a busy Saturday, even the frightening night journeys into the Square, but above all I missed the Rialto and the Lovelies. Jerry had a couple of issues of a magazine called *Peep Show* that I liked to look at, with color pictures of Lovelies almost naked, sometimes on all fours, sometimes not. They often had rugs to lie on, but it was not the same as in the movies.

At first I thought there was no way out of the room, that escape would prove impossible. The crack under the door was too narrow, and though I probably could have gotten down the fire escape, I could never have climbed back up again, and I had no desire to leave for good. Of course I could have just dashed out one day when Jerry opened the door – even with my bad leg I was faster than he was – but that was not what I wanted.

I didn't want to turn on Jerry in that way. I just wanted to know that I could step out whenever I liked, to have that feeling of freedom. And besides, since I had already read all the books in the place at least twice, things could get pretty boring when Jerry was away, a lot of empty afternoons and lonely nights. I had learned from my reading that you can do really awful things when you are bored, things that are bound to make you miserable. In fact you do them in order to *become* miserable, so you won't have to be bored anymore.

I was close to that point when I started work on the Great Hole. I have learned a lot about holes over time, about where you are likely to find one – ill-fitting light fixtures, loose baseboards, and wherever plumbing has been run through walls or floors – and patient exploration inch by inch had convinced me that in Jerry's room there was nothing of the sort. The only hole of substance, if *substance* is the word, was a small crack around the drainpipe of the sink, big enough for a fat mouse, just maybe, but not for even the most emaciated of rats. But as heir and student of the ancient Pembroke diggers I was not daunted, and one day while Jerry was out I set about making the little crack into a big crack. I called it Constructing the Great Hole. It was not that hard, really. Decades of dampness had left the wood spongy and eminently gnawable, and in two short days I had the hole finished, edges nicely smoothed and corners rounded.

Waiting to try it out, I could scarcely contain my excitement. I paced the room like a madman, pulled out books and left them open on the floor – I couldn't keep my mind on the words – or gnawed distractedly, and noisily, at the edges of my box. At one point Jerry threw down the newspaper he was reading and shouted at me, 'For Christsake, Ernie, can't you sit still for one fuckin' minute?' Luckily for our relationship, a little later that afternoon he finally got up, looped on his tie, and left. As soon as I heard the street door open and shut behind him, I lowered myself down. I hated deceiving him like that, but how could I explain? Had I been able to write I might have left him a little note: 'Dear Jerry, I have eaten a hole in your floor and gone for a small walk. Forgive me and don't worry. Love, Ernie.' Or maybe I would have said 'Your Ernie.'

Beneath the floor I found the usual dusty canyons between the joists, but no sign, no tooth marks or tunnels, that the ancestors had ever ventured this far. I followed the sloping drainpipe across the floor to where it connected to a much larger pipe that came up through a dark shaft from far below. I pushed a bit of broken plaster over the edge and listened to it ricocheting off the walls of the shaft, followed by silence from a long way down. I figured this was the same shaft and big black pipe that I had used to climb up out of the basement that fateful day so long ago. I had learned a lot more about plumbing since then, because of all the books I had read under HOME IMPROVEMENT. I knew, for example, that this black pipe was the central drain line into which all the sinks and toilets in the building emptied, which is why it was so big, and that it was connected at the top to a smaller vent pipe in the roof that kept a vacuum from forming when someone flushed a toilet. I loved knowing things like that, even though knowing how a toilet works is not the same as flushing one, a pleasure I could only dimly imagine. *In the Dry Sewers of the Mind: Fantasies of an Armchair Plumber*.

I named this central shaft the Elevator. It went straight down to the basement of Pembroke Books, with stops on every floor. Clambering up and down the shaft was difficult this time, much more difficult than during any previous escalade, and not just because of my damaged leg. I wished it had been just my leg. I often had to pause to catch my breath and I could not hang by my forepaws the way I used to.

That first time down I stopped off at the dentist's office on the second floor. It had two rooms, a waiting room and a drilling room. It had white walls, a linoleum floor, smooth and oily, and a smell like wet newspaper. In the center of the drilling room stood an enormous chair mounted on a steel pedestal, with the drilling instruments hanging from a rack beside it. There was nothing to eat in either room and nothing to read but a pamphlet on tooth decay with color pictures of rotting teeth. I ran my tongue over my own front teeth – no problems there. I shall die, and centuries from now archaeologists – will there still be archaeologists? – will dig up my long yellow teeth and say, 'Look at these, Joe, no cavities.' Like the little boy in the pamphlet who says, smiling brightly, 'Look, Mom, no cavities!' Look, Mom, no cavities. Oh, Flo, funny old Flo, she had her ways, ways that seem almost winning now, her odd gait, stupendous snores, and

funny-tasting milk. No cavities, but memory, corroding, carious. I notice you do not laugh at my jokes anymore. Where has the laughter gone?

Once I had access to the Elevator I fell into the habit of slipping down to the bookstore whenever Jerry was away. I even started taking in shows at the Rialto again. That was the only establishment in the whole neighborhood where business was actually up. I suppose with so many other places closed down and boarded up there was not much for people to do anymore, so they went to the movies. Jerry sometimes got home before me. He could see that I was taking trips on my own, and he clearly did not mind. He treated me like an equal. I would haul myself up through the hole, and Jerry, sitting at the table, would turn and say something like ''Lo, Ernie, how was your walk?' It broke my heart that at those moments I could not say, 'Hi, Jerry, it was swell.'

Now that I could reach the bookstore again, I often hung out there at my usual posts during the day, peering down from the Balloon, looking out from the Balcony, always cautious, hidden, just an eye and the tip of my nose showing, and I sometimes spent whole nights there reading. The bookstore was not at all the happy place it had once seemed. An air of defeat hung over it, and a depressing layer of actual dust as well. Shine obviously had not been using his turkey duster lately. No duster and no whistling, and huge bags like bruises under his eyes. And there were not nearly so many customers as before. People just did not come to this part of town anymore. I guess in their minds it was already gone.

Chapter 11

It was a beautiful September morning when Jerry took me to the Common the first time. We had just finished our usual breakfast of toast and strong coffee, when he reached up and brought the red wagon down from the pinnacle of boxes. I expected him to load up the waffle iron and toaster that had been lying in the closet for weeks, but instead he pulled down the topmost box from the stack, placed it on the floor, and began taking books out of it and piling them in the wagon. I caught sight of the red and yellow cover of *The Nesting*, the dripping red fangs of the giant rat, but there were also many copies of another book, this one with a plain cardboard cover and the pages falling out. He loaded a bunch of each, and then he picked up the wagon and books together in his arms – he was that strong – and I listened to his footsteps stumping down the stairs. I was on the verge of taking the Elevator down to see what was going on in Pembroke Books, when I heard him stump back up. 'Come on, Ernie,' he said. He bent down and scooped. He lifted me onto his shoulder, and, perched there, clinging with one paw to a lock of loose hair, I rode down on him to the sidewalk.

I had ridden on his shoulder before,

around the room, and had always loved it. I liked to pretend that he was a camel and that I was Lawrence. The first time he put me up there, of course, I used the occasion to investigate his temples. After my bad experience with Norman Shine I was not taking anything for granted. But poking around in the undergrowth I had found no crescent ridges, just a reassuringly planar surface somewhat scaly with dandruff, so under Jerry's picture I had posted HONEST and KIND.

Kneeling beside the wagon, Jerry arranged the books in stacks with their titles facing up. I climbed on top of the tallest stack, and he pulled the wagon and the books and me in the warm sunshine all the way down Tremont Street to the Common, which is how I got into the selling side of the book business again.

Only once before had I seen the human world by daylight, in full sunshine, the tall buildings and the leafy trees and the different-colored flowers and the people passing, and that time I had been nearly numb with fear. This time, riding in Jerry's wagon, I had no fear and was able to look into people's faces and up at the trees and feel what I think they call joy. I formulated 'a beautiful world' and let it float off into the blue sky, rippling like a banner. Sure, envy was there too, a taste in my mouth bitter as bile – after all, it was not my world – but I swallowed it. People stared at us as we passed, especially at me, and I looked back at them with my black unblinking eyes.

We set up shop next to the Park Street subway station. Jerry propped a cardboard sign against the

CHERNOW
CLOTHES
MENS - YOUNG &
RAIN CLOTHES
EL NIDO

wagon. It said, in hand-painted letters, BOOK SALE – NEW BOOKS AUTOGRAPHED BY THE AUTHOR. I had, of course, considerable experience with this sort of merchandising effort, and had my advice been asked (if only it could have been!), I would have suggested – tactfully and without playing the know-it-all – that we go out and buttonhole people. I would have said, 'Jerry, boy, you gotta stick the goods under their fat noses, make 'em cough it up just to get you off their back.' I would have been like an old grandfather in a movie giving advice to a kid just setting out in the world (I can see him there with his weak chin and slicked-back hair). But Jerry was not pushy like that. As a businessman he was really terrible. He just leaned against the station wall, smoking one cigarette after another, and waited for people to come up. We did not get very many customers that way.

In the afternoon, after the schools let out, a pack of big kids passed on the other side of Park Street, and they shouted across at us, chanting in unison 'Magoon, Magoon, man from the moon' over and over. Jerry had a lot of self-control – he did not look once in their direction, and you would never have known that he even heard them. Some smaller kids came by too. They came because of me, and they knelt beside the wagon and talked to me in baby talk and tried to coax me into doing tricks as if I were some kind of monkey. One little moron held out his pencil and said, 'Bite this, rat, bite this.' That from a kid who probably stumbled over Dick and Jane – it was really humiliating.

We stayed in that spot most of the day,

right through rush hour, and I got to watch the light changing in the trees, and a few people did buy books, while some others just stopped to talk. Most of the talkers were people like Jerry, with obviously no money for books. They chatted, gossiped about acquaintances they had in common, and joked about being broke. They called each other 'man.' They were all very interested in me, and twice someone asked Jerry if I was tame, and he answered the same both times, 'No, man, he's not tame – he's *civilized.*' And then one of them – Gregory was his name – turned to me as he was leaving and said in a very casual and offhand way, 'So long, man.' That really killed me.

Though almost no one ever knocked on Jerry's door, he knew a lot of friendly people, and they greeted him in passing – 'How's it going, Jerry?' 'Hangin' in there, Jerry?' – even the cops. If you are lonely, I think it helps to be a little crazy as long as you don't overdo it. That's my policy anyway. And in the end, Jerry did make a few sales of *The Nesting*. I think people were attracted by the colorful picture of the giant rat. Whenever somebody bought a copy Jerry autographed it for him and threw in a copy of the other book and his business card as bonuses. The business card said:

E. J. MAGOON
'The smartest man in the world'
Artist Extraordinaire & Extraterrestrial

And that was how he signed his books too. Artist Extraordinaire & Extraterrestrial. People seemed to get a kick out of that. Not everybody, of course, not the real bourgies. Some of them, the ones with the briefcases and suits, just looked at Jerry and smirked. You could see them talking to each other and laughing. They had nice teeth. But whenever their gaze happened to meet mine, I handed them a cold steely stare of such utter contempt that they couldn't stand it. Wiped the smirks right off their smooth faces.

Now and then people stopped to argue with Jerry and try to make him look stupid. They couldn't stand the idea that this old rumpled guy with the wagon was the smartest man in the world. So they would say, 'If you are the smartest man in the world, how come you're selling books out of a wagon?' and other bourgeois idiocies of that sort. Jerry never got mad, though. He very patiently explained to them how in fact he was rich because he was free, because he was not a wage slave and did not bust his ass eight hours a day at some meaningless job. He never raised his voice, he listened to them when they spoke, and sometimes after a while they started having real conversations about serious matters, and you could tell that they had started to like him. Some of them even started telling him how unhappy they were, about their stupid jobs and miserable marriages, and more often than not they ended up buying a book. I guess they hoped it would cheer them up when they got home.

Jerry's other novel did not have a colorful cover. It was really just a stack of loose pages that he had printed himself in a little job shop in the Square. He had turned the loose pages into a book by sandwiching them between two sheets of brown cardboard, punching

holes through the stack, and sewing the whole mess together with white grocery string. It struck me as a pretty shitty-looking affair. But of course I would feel that way, given my background. Using a blue crayon he had written the title by hand on each book in big block letters: THE RESCUE PROJECT.

The story begins on the planet Earth about a hundred years after a vast thermonuclear war between the 'last empires,' the USA and the USSR, has utterly destroyed civilization. Besides pretty much destroying every city and even the small towns, the war had instilled in the surviving rural populations a visceral aversion to all forms of technology, which they saw as somehow responsible for the calamities that had befallen them. There were no more real governments as we know them, only roving bands of warlords and small loose-knit communities of peasant farmers. These farmers tilled the soil with simple wooden plows and mules, and when they plowed at night the radioactive soil glowed in the plow's wake like phosphorus. All over Earth people suffered from unimaginable diseases, including a great many that had not existed before the holocaust, and many of these affected the skin so that most of the people were covered with painful boils. Because of the radiation permeating every inch of the planet, half the children were born damaged – crippled, blind, or imbecilic. The old religions and ideologies, which had played such prominent roles in fomenting the final war, the memory of which was wedged as a recurrent nightmare in the collective unconscious, had been utterly discredited.

But considering how ignorant and brain damaged everyone was, new religions sprang up like daisies. Most did not spread far or last long, however, until the birth of the Castaways.

This new sect was founded by a particularly bloody-minded warlord named John Hunter. He had been raping and pillaging in a small village one day when he was knocked from his horse by a tree limb. Though apparently unhurt, soon afterward he began receiving messages from outer space, and from these he learned that human beings were not originally from Earth at all and had not evolved along with the other species but had arrived as castaways from the wreck of a spaceship. The teachings of this new religion were in perfect harmony with the feeling everyone at that time had of not belonging on the planet. It was hardly the sort of planet anyone would want to belong on. John Hunter told the people that what they needed to do was be rescued, and to do that they needed some way to signal passing spaceships. Of course they had only the simplest technology, no radio or anything like that, so signaling spaceships presented a problem. But John Hunter had the answer. He told them they had to build a pyramid so big it would be visible from space. He spent two years laying it all out with stakes, attracting more and more followers as he went. The base of the pyramid, as it was finally staked out, entirely covered the ancient states of Nebraska and Kansas and much of Missouri, Iowa, and South Dakota.

Wild with fervor, the masses of people set to work, quarrying and transporting stone.

Millions were soon deliriously at labor. In time, engineering skills increased, bureaucracies sprang up. To feed the millions of workers agriculture expanded and intensified. The iron plow, the disk, and the harrow were introduced, and even crude threshing machines. An enormous palace and temple complex was built at each corner of the pyramid for John Hunter and his priests. When John Hunter finally died, he was succeeded by his brilliant and ruthless son Kevin Hunter, and he in turn by the weak and dissipated Wilson Hunter, and so forth until the last leader, the utterly mad Bob Hunter. By that time the labor had gone on for 110 years, and the expense of building the giant pyramid had used up most of the planet's meager resources, while the population was increasingly ravaged by mutation and disease. The last human remnant finally perished in a snowstorm while trying to haul an enormous block of granite from Michigan. Centuries later a space-traveling species actually did land on Earth. They were amazed at the vast unfinished pyramid, and they built a large research center on Earth just to study it, but they never were able to figure out what its purpose was.

I didn't like this story quite as much as *The Nesting*, maybe because there were no rats in it. I liked the generational saga, though, and the way the Hunters, their brains corrupted by power and radiation, got weaker and crazier as time went on. I liked the message. Jerry says people won't publish his books because they are afraid of the message. But I guess that is pretty much my view of life anyway, every day a little weaker and crazier.

Chapter 12

Jerry and I had a lot of good times together. I especially loved our breakfasts, the saucer of strong coffee with milk, and reading the paper together. One day at breakfast we read a long article in the *Globe* about Adolf Eichmann. It showed pictures of trainloads of starving people reaching their skinny arms out through the slats of cattle cars, and piles of emaciated corpses – they had rat faces – and Jerry said it made him ashamed to be human. This was a new idea to me.

I came to really enjoy coffee, and wine too, though never wine in the morning, and not usually in the afternoon either unless it was raining. When suppertime rolled around, Jerry usually fixed things out of cans. Our favorite was Dinty Moore beef stew. Sometimes he cooked some rice to go with it, and at other times, when we were short on cash, rice and soy sauce might be the whole meal. Jerry's mustache was really very bushy and it attracted bits of rice like a magnet when he ate – they seemed to just fly into it. Later on, when I felt secure in our relationship, I used to ferret the bits out with my paws and eat them. That always made him laugh. When he laughed it was easy to imagine that he was the happiest man in the world and not just the smartest.

He did not always go out at night, and sometimes – more and more frequently as the weeks rolled by and the weather turned cold – we spent the evenings sprawled in the old leather armchair together listening to records, lots of Charlie Parker and Billie Holiday. He had a real hi-fi with speakers on both sides, and we drank the red wine that he brought home in jugs from Dawson's Beer and Ale on Cambridge Street. I did not have my own glass, so I sipped from his. I usually sat on the chair arm, and sometimes I got so drunk I fell off and landed in his lap. He laughed, and even though I was not able to laugh I felt good and it was the same as laughing. I had always liked jazz, because of Fred Astaire, and now I grew fond of modern stuff too. We played an L.P. called *No Sun in Venice* over and over, it was so cool and sad, with Milt Jackson on vibes. The vibraphone sounded to me like a lonely rat walking down an empty street in a city made of glass, his paws chiming on the pavement, a clear, high lonely sound that echoed off the buildings.

Sometimes late at night, lying in my box in the dark, on the towel from the Roosevelt Hotel (invisible now beneath the cotton I had pulled out of Stanley), I could still hear the music in my head. I would let it play. I would open my eyes in the dark and think about the Lovelies. I would rub my thoughts against the velvet of their skin, root in the shadowy warmth of their crevices. The longing was so intense – it was a long, hot line running the length of my body. I was never able to fathom how Jerry could bear it, trudging alone through a womanless world, mumbling to himself, big head wagging. Had I been human I would have descended to the streets, accosted the first attractive young one I met, my black eyes glittering above a chinless smile, and I would have beguiled, bought, or ravished. But Jerry just shuffled along in arctic solitude, so lonely he would talk to a rat.

Still, during those good times, at breakfast with the paper or listening to music in the big chair at night, I sometimes experienced a new kind of happiness. It was not like the brilliant gaiety of the old days in the bookstore. It was softer and warmer and almost brown.

Sometimes we let ourselves get carried away and played Bird as loud as it would go, with Jerry doing the drums on the chair arms and me pounding the piano and the whole joint, as they say, jumping. We were so loud that twice the man who lived in the next room – his name was Cyril and he had hair growing out of his nose and sometimes at night we could hear him sobbing – came and beat on the door with the flat of his fat hand and shouted at us to turn it down. And those two times, plus the visit from the fire marshal, were the three times we ever got knocks on our door.

Jerry taught me a lot about jazz, about improvisation and playing the changes and things like that, and later on I worked these into my own music. Sometimes I played while Jerry talked. I wore a white shirt with blue stripes and a garter on my sleeve just like the one Hoagy Carmichael has on in *To Have and Have Not*,

and I carried on a kind of soft musical doodle in the background the way he does in the movie, while Jerry sipped his wine and reminisced about his childhood, which was now very far away in Wilson, North Carolina, and about the time he was in the army. He had joined up right at the beginning of the war, the Second World War. When they found out he was a farm boy they assigned him to the Remount Corps and shipped him off to train mules in Texas, where one day a huge gray one named Peter kicked him in the head. The blow knocked his left eye off to one side, where it stayed. Besides recurrent headaches and double vision, Peter's kick brought with it a little check in the mail every month. 'So you see, Ernie, that fucking mule did me a real favor.' One of the great things about Jerry was the way he could always see the big picture.

And he told me about when he used to live in Los Angeles before the war and had a walk-on part in a movie called *Canyon Riders*. He talked a lot about books too, and the literary scene. He said nobody ever wrote better than Hemingway except Fitzgerald, and he only did it once. And he told me about the exciting things that were happening on 'the Coast' – he meant the West Coast – and he said Boston was a dying city.

I loved it when he talked about the revolution, too, about Joe Hill, Peter Kropotkin, and the Paterson strike. One of his favorite phrases was 'after the revolution.' When people bought his books, he would apologize for taking their money and tell them that books were going to be free after the revolution, a public service like streetlights. He also said Jesus was a

Communist, which caused some of the people to get worked up.

Jerry talked and I listened. Gradually I learned more and more about his life, while he, one can safely say, learned less and less about mine. Due to my natural reticence, he had a free hand with my personality. He could pretty much make me into whomever he wanted, and it was soon painfully clear that when he looked at me what he mainly saw was a cute animal, clownish and a little stupid, something like a very small dog with buckteeth. He had no inkling of my true character, that I was in fact grossly cynical, moderately vicious, and a melancholy genius, or that I had read more books than he had. I loved Jerry, but I feared that what he loved in return was not me but a figment of his imagination. I knew all about being in love with figments. And in my heart I always knew, though I liked to pretend otherwise, that during our evenings together, when he would drink and talk, he was really just talking to himself.

Do I detect a chuckle? You think you have found me out, I suppose. I know, *I know* what I said earlier – that I confessed, testified, and in my perverse way even boasted of my love of cracks, my near-pathological need to hide, my affection for masks. So why, you ask, do I complain now when presented with a new opportunity for concealment, a golden chance to cower unseen behind the impenetrable guise of cuddly pet? Well, I'll tell you why: the difference between assuming a mask, which is always an opportunity for freedom, and having it forced upon one, is the difference between a refuge and a prison. I would have been happy to stump through life wrapped in the furry armor of my pet disguise had I been convinced that I could pop it off whenever I wanted, tear away the adorable cuddle face and leap forth as the creature I knew I was. Hi, Jerry, it's me! I would never have done that, of course, but I liked the idea that I could.

Though I wore the disguise bravely, it always chafed, and sometimes I could not stop myself from gnawing at its edges. When the mood was on me, I liked to defecate in delicate spots, on Jerry's plate or his pillow. He did not care for that at all, though he still failed to get it – instead of nasty little beast, I was just good old Firmin messing up. And once when he was idly scratching me between the ears I turned and gave him a really vicious bite. On his fourth digit. I am sorry about that now. *A Wanderer in the Garden of Regrets.*

When we left the room it was not always to peddle books on the Common. Once we went to the movies. It was early in September, a heavy, smelly, overcast afternoon. Jerry had been on the verge of going out, had the door already open. I was on the table finishing his lunch and reading yesterday's *Globe*. He hesitated, turned, and shot me a look that at the time seemed to say, 'Poor old Ernie, left alone.' Thinking back on it now, though, it seemed more quizzical than that, so maybe it was saying something like, 'Who is this animal anyway?' I prefer it that way. But whichever it was, he came back into the room and scooped me up.

He stuck me in his coat pocket, and off we went to the movies.

The walk to the Rialto was tremendously interesting in a depressing sort of way. I had never done it in the daytime, and now, peeking out from beneath the pocket flap as we bounced along, I was amazed at how daylight ravages, especially when it is dull and gray and not very different from the light that had leaked through the panes of my basement. And it was not just the light. The world with which I thought I was familiar – dark, mysterious, laced with shadow, romantic even, though fraught with danger – had dwindled horribly. A thick haze had starved it of color. Distant views had lost their depth, collapsing into lusterless panels of gray and brown. Neglected buildings, boarded windows, trash-clogged gutters, pinched gray faces. It was all shriveled, sad, and ugly. I couldn't let that bother me, though – I was happy to be striding through the streets of Boston in the pocket of one of the best writers in the world. Of course, it was trudging really, but I say 'striding' because that captures the feeling of the thing.

I had seen every movie the Rialto owned, some of them many times, but I was always game to watch one again. When we reached the ticket window, Jerry shoved me down deep in his pocket, so I was not able to see the posters and had no idea what was showing. I stayed hunkered there while he bought a box of popcorn and a Coke, and then we walked all the way down to the front row. There were only a few people besides us in the whole theater. The movie started up almost right away and as luck would have it, it turned out to be the one movie I really hated, even though it was in Technicolor, which I normally considered a plus. It was called *The Yearling*, and it was a long sentimental saga about a poor boy and his pet deer. I normally don't like stories with animals in them. Jerry, though, clearly loved it, and I realized that he had brought me along because he thought I would love it too, and that made me sad and lonely, though I put on a good face. Besides the deer and a lot of dogs, the movie features a big bear named Old Slewfoot. When he appeared on the screen, Jerry turned to see my reaction. I really hammed it up for him, opening my mouth wide, throwing my forepaws in the air, and falling over backward. I could see he was pleased with that. The movie goes on and on, one affliction after another, until one day, when the deer has eaten all the poor family's corn for the third time, the mother whips out the family shotgun and blasts it. I was glad about that, but I could see Jerry wiping away tears.

We stayed on for the other features. We sat through *Trail to San Antone* and *The Mad Monster*, and it was getting on toward midnight. I hoped they would finish off with Ginger Rogers so Jerry could watch the death and transfiguration scene, but it was Charlie Chan instead. When at midnight the great Chinaman flickered out in midsentence, there was the usual coughing and shuffling in the dark. Then the projector rattled back to life and the angelic assumption began. This time it was *Man-Crazy Kittens*, one of my favorites. Two Lovelies dressed in kitten suits, with adorable little whiskers and ears, were trying to catch a man dressed as a rat, or maybe a mouse. They chased him round and round in a huge house, practically a mansion, but he was too quick for them, vaulting over furniture, climbing drapes, swinging from a chandelier. After a while the kittens tried another tactic. They pretended to give up on the chase. They yawned and stretched and pretended they were going to bed. They started climbing out of their kitten suits, first the shoulders, then one lovely breast. They were so beautiful then. Of course when the big rat sees them naked he can't resist and goes over and mates with them both, one after another and then both together. I am usually deeply disinclined to contemplate Lovelies being mounted by anything as gross as a human male, and I avert my gaze at those moments, but this film was an exception, for obvious reasons. I was not sure if Jerry was going to like it, though. So when they started climbing out of the kitten suits, I looked over to see his reaction. He was fast asleep, head thrown back and mouth agape. Looking around the theater, I could see a few other old guys in the same attitude, and it occurred to me that if you didn't know better, you could mistake Jerry for just another hooch hound on the long slide to nowhere.

Chapter 13

In October Jerry started talking about moving to San Francisco. At first I thought he was just talking, until one day he came home with a Greyhound schedule and spent the evening poring over it, deciding which cities we would visit on the way. On the list, I remember, were Buffalo, Chicago, and Billings. So I took the Elevator down to the bookstore and read everything I could find there about San Francisco, which wasn't much anymore. Jerry was optimistic about Frisco. In fact, I think that was the only time that I ever saw him consistently optimistic about anything, he was such a sad man at heart.

I knew we had to go soon. The Elevator trips down to the store were getting more difficult every day, and I found myself thinking a lot about death. I wondered what would happen if Jerry came back home one night and found me dead, my poor little body stiff and cold. I think my mouth would be slightly open, showing my yellow teeth. (I am usually careful to keep my upper lip pulled well down over them.) What would he do then? Would he pick me up by the tail and drop me in the metal can? And what else *could* he do? Bury me in the Public Garden?

'What ya doing there, buddy?'

'Just burying a rat, officer.'

'Burying a *what?*'

I hated the idea of being picked up by the tail and put in the trash.

But even with the melancholy undertow, these were still good times on the whole, and I like to remember them now, and sometimes I play with them and try to get the sadness out, the old age and the loneliness. I make Jerry young again, with the wavy dark hair and the white-toothed smile he had in the photograph. And I carry us out of the room on Cornhill and fly us high over Boston and across the Mississippi River and the Rocky Mountains and set us down in a bar or coffee shop somewhere in San Francisco – we can see the bay flashing in the background – and sometimes I invite other people to join us, Big Ones like Jack London or Stevenson, and then we really go at it.

I always think everything is going to last forever, but nothing ever does. In fact nothing exists longer than an instant except the things that we hold in memory. I always try to hold on to everything – I would rather die than forget – yet at the same time I was looking forward to San Francisco, to leaving everything behind. And that's life – you can't make sense of it at all. I had been with Jerry six months and seven days. The trees in the Common were dropping their leaves, a red and yellow litter on the grass, sad and crisp, and more and more stores were dying in the Square, their windows and doors boarded over. Trash was everywhere, lying in the streets and gutters or picked up and blown by passing trucks in swirls like leaves. The nights were quieter than before, and I could always hear Jerry when he came stumping home, recognize the footfalls on the stairs. His were slower and heavier and sounded wearier than the footsteps of the other tenants, even those of Cyril, who was fat and had asthma and also took a long time climbing.

One night I was lying awake, half listening for him, the way I usually did, and talking to myself, when I heard the street door open and close, and then the slow familiar steps on the stairs, climbing the first flight and pausing at the landing, the way they always did. Soon, I thought, he will open the door, and if he is not too tanked he will turn on the light and undress and sit on the edge of the bed in his shorts and talk to me a while. He was almost at the top when I heard the noise. I had never heard the sound of someone falling down stairs before, but I knew even while it was still going on that this long tumbling noise was just that sound. Afterward there was no sound at all, just silence settling like a blanket.

I waited for all the doors in the hall to fly open, for the sounds of confused shouts and running steps. But none of those things happened. The sound of Jerry falling shook buildings in Revere and Belmont, and yet no one heard it. As for me, I had no way of getting out into the hall. Even though I knew it was hopeless, I tried frantically to squeeze my way through the crack under the door, my claws scraping loudly against the floor. Then I forced myself to sit still, take a deep breath, and think. I had to find a way to reach Jerry, though what I could do if I reached him I had no idea. So I took the Elevator down to the dentist's office and racing from room to room looked for a way into the hall from there. I knew something awful had happened. All my life I have been burdened, practically crippled, by a monstrous imagination, and all the while I was running this way and that I could see Jerry grotesquely sprawled and shattered, and I could feel him dying over and over. Finally, in desperation I slid and tumbled down the Elevator all the way to the basement, crawled out under the door into the alley, and ran around to the front door under ROOMS, not even caring who saw me. I could not get in that way either. On the door it said PAINLESS DENTIST, and somewhere on the other side of those words, Jerry lay in agony or dead.

So I went back to the bookstore and with great difficulty – I was bruised all over – climbed up into the Balloon and just waited. Shortly after dawn I heard shouts in the street and then the siren. It came, and in a little while it went away, frightened and wailing, to die somewhere in the city west of the Square.

When Shine opened up at nine, they all rushed in, and the heads bobbed and nodded around the desk like apples in a drum of rough water. They talked of the accident a while – they all ran their mouths at once, and the only evident fact to float up from the babble was that Jerry Magoon had fallen down the stairs and been taken unconscious to Mass General – and then they went on to other things, to Alvin's mother's broken hip and the Red Sox.

I went back upstairs to the room. It was already as if he had been gone for years. I couldn't get the top off Skippy. There was a full loaf of Sunshine bread on the table and I gnawed through the plastic and ate some of that. I sat all night in the big chair. To keep my mind off Jerry, I went to Paris to look for the house where Joyce had once lived, but the street signs had melted and I couldn't find it.

I was in the Balloon for opening time the next day. The heads filed in and bobbed. Shine had already been to the hospital to ask after Jerry. They had told him he was unhurt by the fall but had suffered a stroke, was unconscious and being fed through a tube, and they did not expect him to recover. He might die tomorrow, he might die in a year.

'Well,' George said, 'at least he's going to be asleep when he goes. I hope to fuck I die in my sleep, right in the middle of a nice dream.' He was going on to tell about a dream he had had, when Alvin interrupted.

'Yeah, and what if it's in the middle of a fucking nightmare?'

'Well, at least that'll be the end of the nightmare,' Shine said, and he gave a funny little laugh.

'No shit,' Alvin said.

I didn't want to listen to any more sad jokes about death, so I took the Elevator back up and ate another half slice of Sunshine and climbed into the big chair and dreamed Jerry back to life.

I was sure he was never coming home, so I guessed it was O.K. now to root around in his things. When someone is dead, or as good as dead, it's not snooping, it's research. I wanted so much to find the story of the rat. Ever since I had heard him tell Norman about it, I had been sure that somehow that story would have an answer for me. An answer to what? Well, I know it sounds really stupid to say it, but I guess I was still looking for the meaning of my ridiculous life, and I thought that maybe Jerry had found it, or at least was on the trail of it, and that this was the reason he was writing a book about a rat. So a couple of days after he left I climbed up on the table and opened the notebook called 'The Last Big Deal' – he had been writing in it the whole time we were together – and from there I leapt to the bookcase and one by one pulled the other notebooks from the shelf. Each had a title and a date framed in the white rectangle on its cover – they went all the way back to 1952 – 'The Phoenix Dove,' 'The Continuum Project,' 'Dog Star Rising' – twenty-two in total, and all the same: ideas for possible novels, plots partially developed, a character half-sketched, page upon page of notes on background, and now and then a first paragraph or two, worked and reworked, an entire page rewritten to incorporate the change of a single word. A lot of the projected novels seemed to end with the destruction of the planet. I read all day for a week. I had to stop at night, since I could not reach the light switch on the wall. The notebooks were full of wonderful ideas, and during the long dark nights I made some of them come true in my dreams. But there was no story of a rat. The word *rat* did not appear, not even once.

I hung around, eating Sunshine and playing the

piano. I played, and I thought of Mama, who had disappeared, and Norman, who had failed to exist, and always Jerry, who had ceased to exist, and of course myself, who was not sure he wanted to exist. I realized that I had not really known what lonely was before.

Two weeks later Jerry's parents arrived – I had just enough time to dive under the sink before the door opened. It had never occurred to me that an old guy like Jerry could have parents. They were incredibly old, both of them white-haired and bent and ancient, with wrinkled gray skin like gnomes. They had kind faces, especially his mother, who must have been a tall woman once but was now bent way over. They looked like they had come out of a fairy story, and I let the mother come into my thoughts as the Old Woman. They had a dark-haired man with them, who was younger but not truly young, and who I guessed was Jerry's brother, since he had a big head too, and I called him the Youngest Son. The father was very dignified-looking, in a dark suit and tie, and had a broad thin-lipped mouth that did not open often or wide, and whenever it did open to let a few words escape, it quickly clapped shut again like a trap, chopping off the final syllables of each sentence like the tail of a fleeing animal. I named him the King. I watched from the sink while they packed everything up, putting the things that were not in boxes into boxes and taking the things that were in boxes out and looking at them and then putting them back in again. It took them all day. They were not reverential about Jerry's notebooks. They just flipped through a few pages and tossed them in a box.

The only thing that seemed to interest them was a shoe-box full of letters. They all three sat on the bed, the mother sitting between the two men, the box on her lap, and she took the letters one by one from their envelopes and read them aloud, while the other two nodded in recognition. It took me a while to catch on that she was reading back their own words, that these were *their* letters to Jerry – chatty and diffuse, filled with local gossip (who had gotten married or died and whose daughter had run off and whose son had wrecked the brand-new Oldsmobile), littered with redundant little questions ('And who do you think got married last week?'), and pocked with exclamation points, which the mother read out as if they were words ('And Sissy's husband Carl was stopped for speeding and guess who was in the car, it was Ellen Brunson exclamation mark exclamation mark'). And pretty soon all three of them were crying, even the King, his wide mouth turning down. It made him look like a sad clown. And the mother kept reading even while she cried, which made things even worse. Nothing of Jerry's had made them cry, not even his poor ragged underwear and certainly not his pathetic half-empty notebooks. I guess what they were really crying over was themselves and their own lost past. I can't imagine my own family crying over anything. In some ways humans are not very lucky. Peeking out from under the sink at the three of them sitting there on the bed weeping, the mother and the father and the son, I renamed them the Holy Family.

Late that afternoon two men came and took everything away – the books, notebooks, the furniture, even the pots and pans, everything but the garbage can and the piano. I guess they figured nobody could want a rusty garbage can or a kid's broken piano. I didn't care about the can, since I had nothing to throw away, but I was happy about the piano.

Chapter 14

Tired of eating Sunshine, I went back to foraging at the Rialto. They were still showing the same movies, but now there were fewer spectators, if that's what you call them, and less to eat on the floor. I did not have much of an appetite in any case, not for popcorn or Snickers or anything, really. And I did not spend a lot of time in the bookstore anymore. It depressed me and Shine disgusted me. I just dragged around aimlessly, heavy with grief. It was not the kind of grief where you wail and pull your hair. It was more like an encompassing boredom. I was heavy with boredom. Life bored me, literature bored me, even death bored me. Only my little piano did not bore me, and as the weeks dragged by and the book business grew slower and sadder, I spent more time plunking the ivories and singing to myself. Sometimes I forgot to eat, or I didn't forget but it was too much trouble to take the Elevator all the way down and roam the smoke-filled streets to reach the Rialto. I could run my paws down my sides and feel the ribs sticking up like the black keys of a piano. Fewer and fewer customers came to Pembroke Books; even the literary porn business was falling off. And Shine had finally stopped buying – no more estate sales, no more scraping of station-wagon bumpers on the sidewalk. And the ornate antique cash register vanished, sold to a dealer in Back Bay. Now he made change from a gray metal box. And every day there were fewer books on the shelves, lots of empty spaces. No more Dostoyevsky under D, no more Balzac under B. One after another, the Big Ones were catching the last train out. Shine still kept up a brave face, but I remembered the old days and could tell that he was just going through the motions.

The eviction notices were going out a block at a time, and after each mailing, boards went up over more windows, moving vans backed up to doors, and more buildings burned, ruins smoldered, and trash fires flickered in the empty lots. The boarded-up buildings bore yellow signs: KEEP OUT, PROPERTY OF THE CITY OF BOSTON, TRESPASSERS WILL BE PROSECUTED. To the west of the Square itself whole city blocks were missing, you could see a lot of sky, and at night the stars wept. The storekeepers, Alvin and George and several whose names I did not know, bobbed around Shine's desk and drank coffee and shrugged and whined. Alvin said, 'We might as well live in fucking Russia,' and everybody agreed with that and bobbed to it, and then somebody said, 'You can't fight City Hall,' and they all nodded. George said it was stupid to get all worked up over something you can't do anything about anyway, and everybody agreed with that too. Then they started talking about Bernie Ackerman's heart attack and had moved on to ulcers, when Shine, who had not said anything for a while, spoke up in a voice so low they all listened.

'Well, I'm sure as hell going to do *something*,' he said. 'I'm not going to sit on my ass while they haul me out with the furniture.'

They all, of course, wanted to know what he was going to do, but he wouldn't tell them. He just said, 'Something.' And then he said, 'You'll see.'

The thing is, I knew all about the bumps for destructiveness and secretiveness that Shine was concealing on his temples, and I had long ago moved out of my bourgeois phase, so despite my current aversion to his character, I was pretty excited by these words. One thing I was sure of, Norman Shine was not afraid of anybody. I thought of barricades, burning cars overturned in the narrow streets, Molotov cocktails. Or perhaps a great moral struggle like the Negroes in the South I had read about in the *Globe*, a nonviolent sit-down in front of the shop – Shine, Sweat, Vahradyan sitting in the middle of the street, strippers in plaid skirts and cardigans bringing them sandwiches, lots of reporters, an outpouring of public sympathy, a red-faced mayor. Wrong again.

A few days after saying he was going to do something, Shine put up a big handwritten sign in the front window.

FREE BOOKS

ALL YOU CAN CARRY IN 5 MINUTES

So this was what he called doing something. Giving away all the books like this was an act of such generosity and bespoke such exquisite despair that I almost fell in love with him again. Free books, like after the revolution. I wished Jerry were there to see it. The sign had an immediate effect – it's amazing the way freebies can get people moving – and the next five days were chaos. After the *Globe* ran a story on it, so many people showed up for their five-minute raid on the bookstore that policemen on horseback had to be called in to control the crowd, which at one point stretched all the way down Cornhill and around the corner. They came outfitted with paper bags, knapsacks, cardboard boxes, even suitcases, and they loaded up. Some people got carried away and took things they really didn't want, and in the evening after closing time the street was strewn with cast-off books. Shine went out with a paper bag and picked them all up, and the ones that weren't too damaged he put back on the shelves, ready for the next day's stampede, and the rest he threw away. It was exciting at first, and then it was sad. It was sad to walk around the shop at night, a place where I had spent my whole life, my home really, and see all those empty shelves. It was especially sad that Sunday, when it rained. I went down and sat on the red cushion in the chair and looked out the store window and watched the rain run in muddy trickles down the dusty pane. I rested my cheek on a paw and thought of the French poet Paul Verlaine, who wrote a famous poem about the rain falling on a city. When it rains, the poem says, the heart weeps. I knew just what he meant, even though that was Paris, France, and this was Scollay Square in Boston. And that was

when I missed Norman the most. I missed our conversations over coffee, my feet in tassel loafers up on his desk, cozy in the warm, bright shop, while outside the rain was falling. Sometimes I called him back for a visit, and we discussed the case of Shine, his triumphs and his failings, but it wasn't the same as when I had thought he was real.

I began to spend most of every day on my back, all four feet in the air, dreaming and remembering, or else playing the piano, remembering and dreaming. I could see that my dreams were changing. They were getting soft and nostalgic, with a kind of crepuscular flare around the edges, and I didn't have many exciting adventures anymore. I missed the past terribly, even the awful parts. I never forget anything that has happened to me and scarcely anything that I have read, so by that time I had stored up an awful lot of memories. My brain was like a gigantic warehouse – you could get lost in it, lose track of time, peeking into boxes and cases, wandering knee-deep in dust, and not find your way out for days. Sometime shortly after I moved in with Jerry I had begun to play with the past, tweaking it this way and that to make it more like a real story, and I had begun mixing my memories with my dreams. This was probably a mistake, since the more I played with them the more they came to resemble each other, and it was harder and harder for me to tell the things I remembered from the things I had invented. I was now, for example, unsure which of the figures was really Mama, the fat greedy one or the thin, worn sweet one, and whether her name was Flo or Deedee or

Gwendolyn. All the archives existed only in my mind. I had no external check, no diary, no old family friend. How could I verify? All I could do was compare one mental image with another image, equally suspect, and in the end they all got tangled together. My mind was a labyrinth, enticing or terrifying according to my mood. I was losing my footing, and the odd thing was that I didn't care.

Things were ending fast. The ship was sinking, and a week after Shine started tossing books overboard, the Old Howard burned. This was a theater that a long time ago had been famous all across America. I used to trudge by its abandoned hulk on my way to the Rialto. Facade of gray stone, enormous gothic windows, it looked like a church except for the huge sign jutting halfway across the street with THE OLD HOWARD spelled out in lightbulbs. I always hoped they would turn the lights on, but they never did. And it looked like a church for a reason – it had been built as one by the Millerites, a religious sect whose zealots believed that the world was coming to an end. They were right about that, of course. But using the Bible and a lot of suspect math, they had calculated that this would occur on October 22, 1844. In preparation for that event, thousands of true believers sold everything they owned, and then they built a huge fortress of a church in order to have a safe place to be in while it was happening. I loved reading about those people. They were just like me, carrying around with them all the time this huge sense of calamity. When the sun rose on October 23, same as before, they were naturally very disappointed. They sold the church, and I don't know what happened to them then. I guess life must have seemed pretty boring after that. The church became a theater – Edwin Booth played there – a vaudeville house, and finally a strip joint. In 1952, which was still long before my time, the city closed it down for good. They said the shows were lewd and immoral. They objected especially to Sally Keith, who wore tassels on her tits and buttocks that she could spin like airplane propellers in opposite directions. I wish I could have seen that. Afterward, the Howard was just a rat house. Half the rats in the Square lived there.

And now at last the world really was ending, and the Howard was going with it. I was in the Balloon when it burned. Everybody in all the stores rushed out to see the fire. Even Shine went out, just jumped up and left, locking the door behind him. It was the middle of the day and he didn't even put up a 'back soon' sign. If I hadn't known it already, that alone would have told me he was through with the book business. We both were. The sirens wailed off and on the whole afternoon, and when I went by that night only the outer walls were still standing, a smoking ruin, and the street was full of ashy mud. A few people were walking up and down in the mud holding signs that said SAVE THE OLD HOWARD and PRESERVE OUR HERITAGE. It had never looked to me like anything particularly worth saving, and I had never cared for the low-life rats who lived there. Good riddance, I thought. At dawn the ruin was still smoking, when they brought in the huge crane. It had an enormous iron ball on the end of a steel cable, and when the crane moved its arm back and forth the ball began to swing, and it swung higher and higher until, with the ball high on the backswing, the crane suddenly surged forward, and the ball swung forward and down and up and crashed against the side of the Old Howard. The walls must have been really strong, because they couldn't knock them down with the crane. And that was when they sent in the sappers, who put dynamite under the walls and set it off. They did this three times, and each time another wall came crashing down, and a billowing wave of ash and dust rolled down the street for blocks and made the dirty buildings a little bit dirtier.

The next morning General Logue gave the signal, and the acres of heavy machinery began the final assault on the Square, chewing at its edges, eating it up a building at a time. They used cranes with wrecking balls and enormous armored bulldozers whose drivers wore helmets and goggles and rode in steel cages. Each time a building would come crashing down the workers would cheer, and then they loaded the broken pieces into gigantic dump trucks that carted them away. It went on like that for weeks. The streets were full of smoke and dust and the roaring of machines, and now and then an enormous *whump* rattled the store windows, and that was the dynamite.

For rats, peace is a lot like war anyway, so most of them went on with their lives as best they could. The average rat doesn't see much difference between a standing building and a pile of rubble, except that rubble is a better place to hide in. When a building came down, the rats retreated to the ruins of the basements, into broken drains and cracks in the rubble. The *Globe* ran a story about the rats in the ruins, and then Logue sent in white-suited teams to finish them off with poison gas that they pumped into the rubble through hoses. That was when the exodus began in earnest. Every night I passed long lines of them heading out, sometimes whole families together. The *Globe* story had been headlined DEMOLITION UNCOVERS RAT NATION. It called the whole neighborhood 'sleazy and rat infested.'

Infested is an interesting word. Regular people don't infest, couldn't infest if they tried. Nobody infests except fleas, rats, and Jews. When you infest, you are just asking for it. One day I was talking to a man in a bar, when he asked me what I did for a living. I answered, 'I infest.' I thought that was a pretty ironic thing to say, but the man didn't get it. He thought I had said 'I invest' and started asking me for tips on where he should put his money. So I suggested he invest in construction. The shithead.

And then the Rialto closed. I went one night and it was dark. No more Lovelies and no more popcorn. Now I had to scrounge in the streets and ruins like the others, and I started seeing dead rats, sometimes in the middle of the sidewalk. Food was getting scarce, mostly just the leftovers from the workers' lunches, and that was when the horrors began. Some of the starving rats were eating the corpses of their fellows like jackals. I felt ashamed for them, and at the same time I was ashamed at feeling ashamed. Even in the best of times I had not been strong or quick. I limped now, and I was not young anymore. I was hungry all the time. When would I eat corpses? Or would I be crippled by all-too-human scruples, a monster to the last? At night the gutters were full of rats on the run. I thought I glimpsed a couple of my brothers, but I was not sure. It had been a long time, and rats look a lot alike. I sometimes passed in my wanderings whole standing buildings with their facades torn off, all the rooms standing open to the air, some with the furniture still in them and wallpaper on the walls and bathrooms complete with a sink and toilet. They looked like enormous dollhouses.

One morning Shine arrived at the store accompanied by two men in overalls. The men took the desk and chair and all the bookcases that weren't attached to the walls, and they loaded them into a big truck called Mayflower and left. After they had driven away, Shine walked around the shop a while. He did not cry this time. There were still a few books scattered about on the floor and he walked around kicking them. Then he went out and locked the door. I watched him drop the key into his jacket pocket and turn down the street. I never saw him again.

Chapter 15

At that point I still had every intention of following Shine's example, and that of hundreds of my kind. Any minute, I thought, I'm going to beat it out of here. I thought that maybe I would try and find another bookstore somewhere, perhaps across the river in Cambridge, or maybe go to the Common and hook up with one of Jerry's old pals. And yet something I could not explain even to myself, a lethargy or maybe a torpor, kept me from making the move, and every day I put off going. I was still able to scrounge enough food to get by, though never enough to satisfy. The destruction had now reached Brattle Street, and it was clear that in not many days it was going to break over Cornhill. I felt weary and old. A rat's life is short and painful, painful but quickly over, and yet it feels long while it lasts. For days, when I was not hunting up less and less food in the streets, I wandered around the empty store. There wasn't much left to read, just a few boring religious pamphlets. I read them anyway.

Two mornings ago the rain was coming down hard, washing dust and debris off the piles of rubble and forming muddy rivers in the street. On the floor of Pembroke Books, crossed by the shadows of raindrops,

were scattered the remains of several suppers that I had dragged in from the street, morsels and crumbs of food mixed with the orts and offal of the rat life – a greasy wrapper, a greasy strand of bacon rind, peanut shells, pizza crust. The men had stopped working because of the rain, and the roar of the machines had stopped, and now just the rain was roaring. I felt agitated and depressed and spent the morning dragging back and forth in the store, back and forth. The rain did not let up; at noon the day was already growing dark, and I decided to go upstairs and play. It was hard going up the Elevator, and in the silence my breath was loud.

The light was different in the room. I noticed that as soon as I poked my nose up out of the hole. It was not raining, and sunlight was streaming through the open window. The furniture was all back, the bed and the enamel-topped table, the old leather chair, the bookshelves, and all the books. The closet door was ajar, and I saw that it was full of junk again. The rusty trash can was still there and my piano with its chips and scratches. Jerry, I thought, Jerry is coming home. I formulated RESURRECTION and let it glow there. I sat down at the piano and doodled around a little, just to loosen the old fingers, waiting for the footsteps on the stairs; then I went into Cole Porter, 'Miss Otis Regrets' and 'My Heart Belongs to Daddy.' In the end, I would rather be Cole Porter than God. I moved on to Gershwin and 'I Got Rhythm,' and soon I was really getting into it, the piano was jumping and I was bouncing around on the bench and singing at the top of my voice. But even lost in the music as I was, with pictures floating in and out between my ears so fast it made me dizzy, I was aware that someone had entered the room very quietly and was now sitting on the bed behind me. I could feel the listening. I thought, Jerry. I kept right on singing, and while I sang I slowly turned my head and looked.

I had never seen her in color before, and I did not recognize her at first. She was sitting on the bed, hands folded in her lap, rings on her fingers. She had on the black dress she wore in *Swingtime*. I had loved the way she looked then and the way the swirling dress would float up to her hips when she danced. It was the dress that clued me in to who she was. She had changed that much. Only her voice had not changed. 'Gee, that's swell,' she said, 'please don't stop.' So I kept going. I went through the whole piece again, this time with my own variations, and then I stood up and bowed. I signed good-bye zipper, and I could see that she understood. She laughed, and it was not like your laughter. She was still beautiful, even though I could see that something heavy, time or sadness, had pooled in vague loops below her chin and crinkled the corners of her eyes. They were blue.

I went to the window. It was dark outside. She came over and stood behind me. I could feel her looking. I could feel the black dress like a cloud behind me. I was aware of being tall.

From the window I looked out over a vast plain of rubble, as in the pictures of Hiroshima, reaching all the way to the horizon. I

was surprised the destruction had gone so far; it had not been planned that way. From the alley below my window to where it crashed into the sky lay a rocky prairie. It had been made by breaking buildings, breaking them up into windows, doors, stair treads, boards, bricks, doorknobs, and breaking these in turn into pieces so small they did not even have names, and spreading all of it out and grinding it down and running it over until it had no meaning left and was nothing but rubble and emptiness, and in the middle of it all stood the Casino Theater. It was flooded with light, and you could see the scars on its sides where the adjacent buildings had been torn away. With no street to be on, it was a building with no address. I named it the Last Thing Standing. On each side of the ticket window were the two angels I had first seen the night Mama took Luweena and me on orientation. They were still wearing black rectangles across their breasts and crotches, one foot lifted as if dancing. Music, faint and tinny, like something made by a music box, was coming from the building, wafting across the rubble. It was incredibly sad, the nostalgic down-at-the-heels sadness of an old circus on the edge of bankruptcy. The entire theater was illuminated and on the marquee in white running lights with no bulb missing were the words THE NEXT BIG DEAL and below that ALL TICKETS HALF PRICE.

They were lining up at the ticket window, three or four abreast, the line snaking across the rubble field. And people were still arriving by ones and twos, walking in out of the darkness from every direction.

They carried bundles and suitcases, and some led children by the hand. They were happy to be approaching the lighted area around the theater, but no one was running, and they made no sound at all, or only small sounds, whimperings and scrapings and the like, that were drowned by the music, faint as it was. Hundreds and hundreds of people in a line shuffling silently forward between the angels, who each raised one foot as if dancing. I posted REFUGEES beneath the picture. And I thought, Jerry would have gotten a kick out of this.

Ginger was standing beside me at the window. I was wondering if she could see it too, when she said, 'That's where I'm working. Every night I take my clothes off in a number called "The Dance at the End of the World." It drives 'em crazy.'

I thought, *You* work as a stripper?

'Only as a night job.'

So you can read my thoughts.

'Your thoughts and more than your thoughts – your beliefs and desires.'

I don't believe anything.

'You believe you are a rat.'

The music grew suddenly louder, swelling to a slow swing tune with lots of brass.

'Here, this is for you,' she said. She handed me a box of popcorn. The box was red and white and had a picture of a clown on it with a geyser of popcorn erupting from the top of his hat.

And there, in the middle of Jerry's old room, she began to dance. I had never seen her dance like that, except maybe sometimes in my head. It was the sort of stepless dance the Lovelies did in the Rialto after midnight, a bump and grind, hips undulating to the beat, slow and hard. I climbed up into the armchair with my popcorn, and I watched. She stepped from her dress, and picking it up on the toe of her foot, sent it sailing into a corner. She had nothing on underneath. She danced naked. She caressed the rat nest of fur between her legs. Her eyes were half-closed, her lips parted. I have never really understood this expression, though I think it indicates a special kind of human longing. I was sorry we did not have a rug so she could do that part too. And then she swooped upon me, picked me up, and we danced together. She danced and I floated. She held me between her breasts. I buried my head in her smell; it was like wet leather. We swayed and whirled; it was like flying. And the walls of the room moved out, like a stage set, and we were dancing in a huge white place. I closed my eyes and imagined we were flying over the city and all the people in the streets were looking up and pointing. They had never seen anything like it, a naked angel carrying a rat. We danced a long time, we danced faster, the music grew louder, it was madness and frenzy. Then suddenly it stopped. The silence came crashing in and the walls rushed back into place. She let herself fall backward onto the bed. She was laughing, still holding me to her. I could feel her chest rise and fall beneath me. And I felt the grip of her fingers loosen on my back, and when I looked up her eyes were shut. I wriggled from her grip and slowly crept toward her face, smelling the smell of her neck and then the warm smell of her breath. Little diamonds of sweat glistened on her upper lip, and I drank them one by one. They were salty. I knew from my reading that this was also the taste of tears.

She sat up, pitching me backward onto the bed.

'Time's up,' she said. She crossed the room to where she had kicked her dress. She bent over and I saw she was slipping her legs into black pants.

What happened to the dress?

She didn't answer. After the black trousers came a white shirt and then a black business jacket to match the trousers. She was leaving. Had I been a man I could have groveled at her feet, clung to her ankles and wept. I didn't want her to go, ever.

Don't go.

Her face grew hard. 'Don't be stupid, Firmin. This really is the end.'

No. I'll make you stay. Watch this.

I did all my tricks for her. I couldn't do a full flip anymore because of my bad leg and my old age and my heavy head, and each time I tried I landed on my back, which for laughs turned out to be just as good. Then I went to a book and pretended to read. She laughed. But she was leaving anyway. Through the window I could see the dawn breaking.

'The job at the Casino is night work. My day job is with the city.'

You work for *them?* But, Ginger, you can't do that. They are the enemy.

'Everyone has two jobs, Firmin, a day job and a

night job, because everyone has two sides, a dark and a light. You do, they do, I do. No one can escape it.'

Then I noticed an enormous briefcase on the metal table. She snapped it open and riffled through a sheaf of official-looking papers, finally pulling one out and holding it toward me. 'Everyone is his own enemy, Firmin, you should know that by now.'

She laid the paper open on the floor in front of me. I stood on it and read, NOTICE OF EVICTION.

I let my gaze run down the page to the final paragraph. 'And pursuant thereof, the Rat Firmin, trespasser, vagabond, bum, pedant, voyeur, gnawer of books, ridiculous dreamer, liar, windbag, and pervert, is hereby evicted from this planet.' It was signed by General Logue himself.

Why do you give me this? It's an eviction notice. 'Or an invitation. It's up to you.'

She left, pulling the door shut behind her. I could hear the sharp click of the latch, followed by the long descending clicks of her heels going down the stairs. There was a soft curving sound that was the street door opening, and then the noise, growing suddenly louder, of a bulldozer moving up Cornhill, its steel treads clicking.

I scrambled up on the armchair and stretched out on my back, four feet in the air. I closed my eyes. I did more than close them, I scrunched them up. I hauled out my little telescope and looked for Mama. I started to tell the story of my life. It began, 'This is the saddest story I ever heard.' I lay there all morning, the sentences arriving like caravans out of the desert, bringing

pictures. I wondered what I was going to call it. But the story kept getting mixed up with water. At first it was glasses of water popping up in the wrong places, then it was buckets of water, and finally it was rivers and torrents of water, the poor camels upside down in it, knobby legs flailing as their humps dragged them to the bottom. I was terribly thirsty. Maybe it was the salt of her sweat that made me feel this way, but I knew I had to find water. I climbed out of the chair where I would gladly have spent the rest of my life had there been water and took the Elevator down. I was weaker than I had thought, and several times I almost fell. I wondered whether I could ever get back up.

I got off at the store. The front window was smashed and the rain had left a thin puddle at the edge of the sill. I drank it all and then licked the dampness from the big pieces of broken glass. I crawled into the corner where the cash register used to stand and fell asleep. For the first time in weeks I did not dream anything. Late that afternoon I was awakened by a tremendous jolt, followed by a shower of dust and plaster. I opened my eyes again. A narrow fissure had opened in the wall above me. I poked my head into it and looked out at what was left of our street. Most of the buildings that had lined the other side were gone, and in their place rose mountains of rubble. A huge yellow machine, mud splattered and growling, was roaming like a dinosaur through the canyons. Its name was Caterpillar. As I watched, it opened an enormous mouth and began to chew up a concrete pillar that had once been part of the back wall of Dawson's Beer and Ale, the bits and

SHINE
Books

pieces tumbling from its jaws like rice from a baby's mouth. A *Window on the End of the World*. After a few minutes I turned away. I had spent a lifetime looking at the world through cracks, and I was sick of it.

Yet even as I turned from that fissure, with its view of the dying present, it was only to face another, this one a crack in time. Memories were pouring through it like an ocean.

And I was thirsty again. I went down to the basement, using the steps this time, to see if there was any water left in the toilet. By the time I had reached the bottom step the whole building was shaking. The concrete floor seemed to undulate beneath my feet. The fluorescent light hanging from the ceiling, which had flickered and hummed overhead while I, so long ago, just yesterday, had chewed and read my way toward another kind of light, had flickered out weeks ago. Now it was swinging like a dark pendulum, swinging and shaking, to the rhythm of the great waves of destruction breaking over Cornhill. I passed beneath it, and an instant later it crashed to the floor behind me. Curved bits of milky glass flew across the room, some of them falling on my head and back like a dry rain. Rat's feet over broken glass, quiet and meaningless. The door under RESTROOM was open and the toilet bowl lay in two pieces on the floor. No water there. In my dry cellar. Ginger was right, this really was the end. I thought of my little piano up on the top floor, crushed beneath falling beams. There was nothing I could do to save it now. When the first beam struck it, I imagined it giving forth a last tiny sound of its own, and no one would hear it. I thought about climbing to the top of one of the giant dollhouses and throwing myself off, but I didn't think I weighed enough to die that way. I would just float to the ground like a leaf. I mention those thoughts because that was what was going through my head when I caught sight of the book. It was jammed under the water heater, just a corner showing. I recognized it right away and went over and pulled it out. I could see the marks of my baby teeth on the cover, and some of the torn pages still showed the prints of Flo's dirty paws where she had braced herself for tearing.

And then I was sure.

It took a long time and all my strength to work the book around behind the heater and into what was left of our old nest in the corner, a few piles of soiled confetti with almost no smell left. Once in there I could scarcely hear the sounds of the world. The roar of trucks became the wind. The crashes and booms of falling walls were the surf beating on black rocks. And the sirens and car horns became the sad calls of seabirds. It was time to go. Jerry used to say that if you didn't want to live your life over again, then you had wasted it. I don't know. Even though I consider myself lucky to have lived the life I did, I would not like to be that lucky twice. I tore off a piece from the back of the book and folded it over and over. It became a wad. I made myself a little dip in the confetti, and holding the wad down with my forepaws, I read what was written on the top, and the words rang in my ears like trumpets: 'Ho hang! Hang ho! And the clash of our cries till we spring to be free.' I turned around once in my nest. I unfolded the wad, unfolding it all the way out till it was once more a piece from a page, a page from a book, a book from a man. I unfolded it all the way out and I read: 'But I'm loothing them that's here and all I lothe. Loonely in me loneness. For all their faults. I am passing out. o bitter ending! They'll never see. Nor know. Nor miss me. And it's old and old it's sad and old it's sad and weary.' I stared at the words and they did not swim or blur. Rats have no tears. Dry and cold was the world and beautiful the words. Words of good-bye and farewell, farewell and so long, from the little one and the Big One. I folded the passage up again and I ate it.